First American Edition 2020
Kane Miller, A Division of EDC Publishing

Text © Alesha Dixon, 2019
Cover design by Dradog
Inside illustrations by Rob Parkinson in the style of James Lancett
represented by the Bright Agency © Scholastic, 2019
The right of Alesha Dixon to be identified as
the author of this Work has been asserted by her.

First published in the UK by Scholastic Ltd., 2019
This edition published under license from Scholastic Ltd.

For information contact:
Kane Miller, A Division of EDC Publishing
PO Box 470663
Tulsa, OK 74147-0663
www.kanemiller.com
www.usbornebooksandmore.com
www.edcpub.com

Library of Congress Control Number: 2019946994
Printed in and bound in the United States of America
2 3 4 5 6 7 8 9 10
ISBN: 978-1-68464-081-2

SUPERPOWER SHOWDOWN

ALESHA DIXON

In collaboration with Katy Birchall
Illustrated by James Lancett

Kane Miller
A DIVISION OF EDC PUBLISHING

I dedicate this book to all the young readers

who have loved being a part of Aurora Beam's world!

You have all inspired me and I couldn't have done it

without you, so from the bottom of my heart:

thank you!

THE WEEKLY

CROWN T

STILL AT

Special report by Olive Folio

The thief who stole the Imperial State Crown is yet to be caught, Scotland Yard has said today. The Metropolitan Police issued a statement this morning detailing the ongoing investigation into the man who impersonated a butler at Buckingham Palace and stole the crown jewels during an award

HIEF
ARGE!

...eremony honoring superhero Lightning Girl and her friends, the Bright Sparks. So far, few details have been revealed of the incident. There are unconfirmed rumors that Her Majesty the Queen has enlisted the help of Lightning Girl to find the thief. We have contacted Lightning Girl for comment.

THE DAIL

DARKNESS

OVER

Special report by Henry Nib

The skies have grown darker over London and its neighboring counties, top scientists confirmed today. After weeks of even more than usual overcast and dim skies above the Southeast, studies prove the sk is forty-seven percent darker tha

Y SCOPE

DESCENDS

LONDON!

...as this time last year. "It is remarkable," said Gareth Gale, a meteorologist based in Essex. "The cause of these dark skies is still to be explained. The odd thing is, it's not just London. I have heard reports of unusually dark skies in other regions, also."

At a press conference this morning, the prime minister assured the nation that she had "the best people looking into this strange but likely harmless phenomenon, and there is no need for anyone to panic."

As a superhero, I have faced many challenges in my life.

For example, when I found out I was able to shoot light beams from my hands and had to keep it a secret. Or when I had to stop my science teacher, who turned out to be a bad guy in disguise, from stealing a precious stone that happened to be the source of all my powers. And then there was the time he returned to steal it from right under my nose at a top secret global gathering of superheroes.

Not to mention last term when I discovered that my mum's cousin, Darek Vermore, had kidnapped my brother and was in fact an evil mastermind trying to steal the stone for himself, acting on years of simmering jealousy over the powers of the Beam family's women.

So, yeah, you could say that I've found myself in a few tight spots.

But there has NEVER been a moment when I've been more terrified than this one right here.

Ever.

The back of my neck was damp with cold sweat. I felt sick to my stomach. I tried to move away, but I felt frozen to the spot. Any minute now, the whole world would be expecting me, Lightning Girl, to go out *there*. I gulped.

I can't do this. I want to run away. What am I going to do? I can't do it!

"Aurora?"

I jumped about five feet in the air at my best friend's voice.

"Kizzy!" I yelped, gripping my chest. "You nearly gave me a heart attack!"

She giggled. "Sorry," she said, fiddling with her headset. "I thought I'd come and check that you were OK. You've been standing here for about five minutes staring through that tiny gap in the curtain at the audience filing in, and I'm not sure I've seen you blink once."

"I was just ... uh ... checking that the curtains were sturdy," I said hurriedly, pretending to examine the material hanging in front of me. "Yep, looks like everything's in order. The stage is safe. The show can go on and all that."

I laughed nervously. Kizzy did not look convinced.

"You were checking the sturdiness of the curtains," she said slowly.

She folded her arms and raised her eyebrows to give me the look that only Kizzy can do. It's her you're-not-fooling-anyone-but-especially-not-me-the-smartest-kid-in-the-school look.

"Are you nervous?" she continued. "Are you worried about stage fright?"

"Stage fright? Please!" I laughed in a VERY over-the-top manner. "I have come face-to-face with bad guys trying to take over the world! And you think I'm scared of appearing in a school fashion show? HA!"

Kizzy didn't say anything. She just carried on giving me that look. Swallowing the lump in my throat, my eyes flickered toward the small crack in the stage curtains. Every seat in the school theater was filled and the noise was getting louder and louder, as the audience chatted excitedly before the show began.

"OK, fine," I squeaked, my voice at a higher pitch than it had ever been before. "I may be a

TINY bit nervous."

Kizzy smiled warmly at me and linked her arm through mine to lead me away from the curtains and to the side of the stage where everyone else was getting ready.

"Don't worry, Lightning Girl," Kizzy whispered. "I won't tell anyone."

It was our friend Georgie's idea to do a big school fashion show to raise money for charity. The teachers had all thought it was a brilliant idea and asked any budding designers to help her organize it. When Georgie asked me if I would join our friend Suzie and several other classmates to be in the show, I didn't hesitate to say yes because (a) she's one of my best friends and I wanted to support her and (b) I had a cold at the time and clearly the medicine had gone to my head and I wasn't thinking straight.

WHY DID I VOLUNTEER TO PUT MYSELF THROUGH THIS TORTURE?

"You look great, Aurora." Georgie smiled as Kizzy led me toward her. "Do you like your outfit?"

"I really do. Thanks, Georgie," I replied honestly as she came over to tweak my jacket sleeve and check that the rest of me was in order.

No matter how nervous I was to go out on stage, I had to admit that my outfit was the coolest thing I'd ever worn. It was a gold sequin, Lightning-Girl-branded jacket, with black jeans that had lightning bolts sewn down the sides. Georgie had designed and made it herself, just like she had my Lightning Girl sneakers, sunglasses and denim jacket. There were a lot of photographers from newspapers and magazines in the audience, thanks to some of the other students tweeting that I was in the show, so Georgie was extra worried about my outfit being perfect. She knew there was a chance it would be online everywhere as soon as I walked out onto the stage.

I still hadn't really gotten used to the fame side of things. Ever since the world found out that the other women in my family and I had superpowers, the press had followed me a lot. I don't know why they were so keen on getting photographs of me just walking my dog, Kimmy, or heading to school. Yesterday, there was a photo online of me yawning with the headline: *LIGHTNING GIRL YAWNS! IS SHE TIRED FROM WORKING ON THE CROWN JEWEL CASE?!*

And, let me tell you, that picture confirmed I do NOT look my best when I'm yawning.

My older brother, Alexis, said it reminded him of the picture he took during summer vacation of one of my grandmother's alpacas yawning.

A comment that filled me with confidence.

I was just glad I had the Bright Sparks at my side – when my classmates Kizzy, Georgie, Suzie and Fred witnessed my superpowers on a school trip, back when the whole thing was a secret, they decided to form a superhero club and call themselves the Bright Sparks, ready to help me if I ever got into trouble. Which, so far, has been quite often.

At Christmas, we were all awarded medals by the Queen at Buckingham Palace for our bravery in stopping Darek Vermore from extracting the Beam family powers from the most precious stone in the world, the Light of the World. The stone is the source of my family's powers of light and I discovered that, not only do I have superpowers from the stone, I'm its chosen guardian. It's my job to protect it.

Kind of a lot to take in, really.

Anyway, we had this big showdown on the rooftop of Darek's tech business headquarters in London, Vermore Enterprises. Thanks to the Bright Sparks who came to my rescue, the Light of the World is now safe and sound, and Darek is in jail. But Mr. Mercury, his right-hand man, managed to escape.

"Are you sure you don't want me to cartwheel down the catwalk twice?" Suzie asked, checking her blond ponytail in a mirror. "I'm not sure once will be enough."

Unlike me, there was no chance that Suzie was worried about stage fright. She's an amazing gymnast and used to performing in front of an audience. For the show, Georgie had designed a personalized blue-and-silver sparkling leotard for her, and Suzie loved it so much that she had already decided to wear it for the national competitions this year as the reigning champion.

"Only once down the catwalk, please, Suzie," Georgie instructed, with a knowing smile to me and Kizzy. "Everyone else has to get down the catwalk, too, and we've rehearsed the perfect timing to the music. That is" – Georgie grimaced – "if Fred remembers to play the right music this time."

Kizzy giggled and put a finger to her headset before speaking into the microphone. Fred had volunteered to be in charge of lighting and sound for the show.

"I hope you heard that, Fred," she said, winking at Georgie. There was a moment's pause as she listened to his reply from the sound and lighting box before she gave a sharp nod. "He says not to worry. He's got it all under control."

She then hesitated and rolled her eyes, speaking again into her headset. "No, Fred, I'm not going to repeat that. You had better not. Suzie would kill you."

"What did he say?" Suzie demanded, hands on her hips.

"He said he plans on shutting down the lights as soon as you step out onto the stage." Kizzy laughed as Suzie's eyes narrowed to slits. "But he's only joking, I promise."

"Tell him that if he does that or gets anything wrong, I'll let slip to Miss Nimble that it was him who stole that man's wig in Paris on the school trip," Suzie seethed.

"Don't worry, Suzie," Georgie said firmly. "If Fred does anything to ruin my fashion show, I'll make sure he's in BIG trouble."

Kizzy nodded. "Fred says he heard that, and this show is going to go off without a hitch." She checked her watch and then clapped her hands together excitedly. "Right, it's time!"

At Kizzy's signal, there was chaos backstage

as everyone got into position for the start of the show. Being the most organized person I've ever met, it made sense that Kizzy was the stage manager, but even I had been amazed at how smoothly she'd kept everything running.

"Good luck, everyone!" she whispered.

The audience fell into silence as the lights over their heads went down, the spotlights came up on stage and the curtains drew back in time to the blaring music. Georgie gave Suzie a thumbs-up.

"The stage is yours!" she said, beaming at her with excitement and nerves.

Taking a deep breath and rolling her shoulders back, Suzie strutted onto stage to a huge round of applause. Lifting her arms high above her head, she then launched forward down the catwalk in a series of cartwheels and flips. The audience gasped in amazement.

Kizzy smiled, as we watched from the wings. "She really looks like she belongs out there," she said proudly.

I nodded, too nervous to say anything.

"You're going to be brilliant, Aurora," Kizzy said encouragingly, noting my expression. "Here, I thought you might need these."

She held out my Lightning Girl sunglasses.

"They'll help you feel more comfortable and a little more hidden." She grinned as I gratefully took them. "And Georgie has given permission for you to wear them. In fact, she thinks they complete the outfit."

Georgie was busy applauding Suzie as she cartwheeled her way back down the catwalk.

"Thanks, Kizzy," I said, putting them on. "What would I do without you?"

"You ready?" she asked, as Suzie sauntered back toward us, blowing kisses at her adoring audience. "Go do your thing, Lightning Girl!"

With a little nudge from Kizzy and a big encouraging smile from Georgie, I stumbled onto the stage and began walking down the catwalk. Another round of applause filled the hall and a hundred flash bulbs went off as the reporters immediately yelled, "It's her! It's Lightning Girl!" and tried to get the perfect shot.

All the bright lights and noise made my whole body feel like jelly as the nerves kicked in harder, and I tried my

best to focus on not falling over. But I got a boost of confidence when I spotted my family up on their feet, cheering me on.

Mum and Dad were beaming with pride, whooping louder than anyone else. Alexis had even bothered to put his phone away so that he could cheer along, while Clara, my eight-year-old sister who has the brain of a Cambridge graduate, had stacked some heavy science books on her chair, so she could stand on them and be the tallest in the crowd, waving madly at me as I walked past.

Then, disaster struck.

I was walking as carefully as possible back down the catwalk, thrilled that my time in the spotlight was almost at an end, when suddenly we were plunged into darkness.

Everything went black as the lights in the building shut down. The music switched off and there was a ripple of gasps and shouts of "What's going on?" from the audience. Unable to see a thing, I froze to the spot, terrified of walking in the wrong direction and falling off the stage.

Knowing that Fred would never *really* try to sabotage his friend's show, I was wondering what it could be when someone in the audience yelled, "Apparently all the lights in the town have gone out."

Another freak blackout. It was happening all over the world. Lights would suddenly fade, causing absolute chaos. People had started reporting the skies growing darker, too. Something was going on. Something bad.

"Aurora!" I suddenly heard Kizzy shout. "Use your powers! You can save the show!"

She was right! Why hadn't I thought of that? I quickly closed my eyes and concentrated on my powers. I felt that familiar tingle of warmth running through my veins and then my hands began to glow. Holding my hands up, I cried, "**SHABEAM!!**" (*Technically*, I don't need to shout anything to summon my powers, but I thought it might add a bit of flair to the show.) Sparks flew from my fingertips and glittering beams came blasting out of my palms, bathing the stage in a bright light.

The crowd cheered, and I saw Fred, above them in the technicians' box, punch the air before pressing a button to blare out the music. The next model came out onto the stage and the show was able to continue as I pointed one hand in his direction, my light beam acting as his own personal spotlight.

Making sure I didn't grow tired, Mum jumped up on stage next to me and used her powers too, blasting out her light beams from her hands to help illuminate the room. The

building lights finally came back on to a loud cheer from the audience and I was able to exit the stage pronto.

"Phew!" I said, running off stage toward Kizzy. "That was lucky! I wonder why these blackouts keep happening. It's so weird that—"

"Um ... Aurora?" Kizzy interrupted me

nervously. "There are some people here to see you."

She gestured behind her. A man and a woman, dressed in black suits, wearing sunglasses and earpieces, were standing in the wings, being stared at by everyone waiting to go on stage.

"Aurora Beam?" the woman said as I approached them.

"Yes." I gulped. "That's me."

"You need to come with us," the man said, peering at me over his sunglasses. "The Queen would like a word."

I was led to a row of sleek black cars parked outside the school. The door of one opened and someone with bright-pink hair emerged from the back seat.

"Nanny Beam!" I cried, running to give her a big hug.

"Hello, Aurora! How was the show? Sorry I missed it." She held open the car door for me. "Hop in and you can tell me all about it on the way to see the Queen."

Nanny Beam is the coolest grandmother

on the planet for several reasons. Firstly, she has superpowers, just like mine and Mum's, so that's a pretty good start. Secondly, she also happens to be the head of MI5. Yeah. My grandmother is a spy. And not just any spy. The HEAD spy. Which is why, when she came to pick me up from a school fashion show, she had a load of MI5 agents in tow and why she just so happens to be old friends with the Queen. And thirdly, she's the nicest person and she almost never tells me off, even when I do silly things. Like the other day when she told me not to touch this weird extra button she had on her phone and I pressed it anyway.

About eight MI5 agents came bursting through the ceiling, thinking she was under attack and had activated an emergency alarm.

It was very intense.

Anyway, Nanny Beam has had a tough time of it recently, what with her nephew Darek turning out to be this horrible bad guy who wasn't using his technology business for good, as we thought. He had in fact tricked Nanny Beam and infiltrated his way into MI5 so that he could get his hands on the Light of the World.

It was hard for Nanny Beam because she really did care about Darek. Her brother, Nolan, died years ago in this awful light explosion in a warehouse while he was trying to do the exact same thing and extract powers from a precious stone: the Jewel of Truth and Nobility.

Nanny Beam and Nolan didn't exactly see eye to eye, considering his line of work, but she had done her best to have a good relationship with his son, to make up for what had gone down between her and Nolan before his death. She truly believed that Darek was different than his father and it must have been really sad for her to discover that he had made all the same mistakes.

"Why does the Queen want to see me?" I asked, climbing into the car at her request and admiring the posh leather seats. "Have you found Mr. Mercury and the crown?"

The last time anyone had seen Mr. Mercury was the day the Bright Sparks and I got our medals from the Queen. None of us knew that he had been in Buckingham Palace the whole time masquerading as Joe, one of the Queen's butlers.

If there was one thing Mr. Mercury was good at, it was disguise. He used to be known as the Blackout Burglar – he'd be incognito and then shut off all the power in buildings, stealing things during the blackout. He'd tried to do just that during my dad's last exhibition at the Natural History Museum. He had in fact been trying to steal the Light of the World for Darek.

I still can't get my head round the fact that

he's been working for Darek Vermore all this time. It made a lot of sense though, when I really thought about it. Mr. Mercury may be a master of disguise, but he was never going to be the brains of the operation.

That's what makes his latest steal all the stranger.

That day in Buckingham Palace, the day we got our medals, Joe revealed himself to be Mr. Mercury wearing a blond wig, prosthetic chin, nose *and* forehead, and took off with the Imperial State Crown.

A crown that is a lot more precious than anybody realizes.

"We haven't found Mr. Mercury yet, but he can't hide forever," Nanny Beam replied, getting in next to me and pulling her phone out of her pocket. "I'll just text your mother and let her know that I'm borrowing you for an hour or so."

"Where are we going? Buckingham Palace?"

"Her Majesty thought a little outing would be a lot more fun. The Queen has a very adventurous spirit. And, since she found out that Mr. Mercury had been posing as one of her butlers for rather a long time, she's not entirely sure who to trust in the palace. We thought it would be better to chat somewhere else."

"So, how come she wants to see me?" I asked.

"She wants to discuss what happened at the medal ceremony with you properly. She realizes that because it was Christmas and she had a rather hectic schedule, we never got a chance to sit down, just us three, and go through everything. She wants to see how you are."

"That's nice of her," I said, glancing down at my sequin jacket. "Do you think she'll mind that I haven't exactly dressed knowing I was meeting the Queen today?"

Nanny Beam smiled. "Trust me, she'll think you look fantastic."

As the car sped toward London from our village in Hertfordshire, my stomach filled with butterflies at the idea of seeing the Queen again. Nanny Beam changed the subject to the fashion show and asked after the Bright Sparks, before telling me all about her alpacas and how each one was doing. Nanny Beam lives in a cottage in Cornwall and has dozens of rescue animals there, including chickens that wander freely about the house. If you stay in the guest room, you often wake up to find one sitting on your chest, peering curiously at you and clucking away.

By the time we reached central London, Nanny Beam had gone through every animal on her farm and made me laugh so much by recounting how one of her alpacas stowed away in the postman's delivery van that I had almost forgotten why I was in the car.

The nerves came flooding back when the car came to a stop and Nanny Beam said, "Ah, we're here. The Queen is already waiting for us."

One of the serious-looking agents opened the door for me and I stepped out into a busy tourist spot.

"Hyde Park!" I exclaimed, dodging out of the way of someone coming past on a skateboard.

"Yes," Nanny Beam said, gesturing for me to follow her. "This way!"

"I thought we'd be going somewhere private," I said, falling into step alongside her. "This is one of the busiest places in the city."

"You should see it in the summer. It is a lot busier then; this is rather quiet for Hyde Park. Besides, you'll often find that the busier the place, the more private it can be."

Nanny Beam came to a stop at the Serpentine

Lake in the middle of the park.

"Fancy a pedal boat ride?" she asked cheerily.

"Um, no thanks, we shouldn't really keep the Queen waiting," I said, looking at her as though she was mad. "And look at the sign. Boating on the Serpentine doesn't open until April."

She glanced at someone over my shoulder, a smile creeping across her face. I turned to see a pedal boat bobbing on the water with the Queen sitting in it, wearing a warm coat and sunglasses.

"Hello, Aurora!" She waved, before checking that her headscarf was in place. "Won't you join me? Love your jacket by the way!"

My mouth dropped to the floor.

"We pulled a few strings. Now, like you said," Nanny Beam chuckled, prodding me in the back, "you shouldn't really keep the Queen waiting."

"Aren't you coming?" I asked Nanny Beam, still staring at the lone pedal boat and the Queen looking absolutely delighted to be in it.

"There's only room for two in each pedal boat. Go and have a good chat; I have some work to do. I'll be here after you've been for a spin around the lake."

She ushered me toward the water and, after I greeted the Queen with a very wobbly curtsy, one of the agents helped me to climb into the pedal boat without tipping it over and causing the Queen to fall into the Serpentine. I could see the potential headlines the next day: LIGHTNING GIRL ALMOST CAUSES QUEEN TO DROWN IN PEDAL BOAT SCANDAL!

"Isn't this wonderful?" the Queen said, once I was in. "Let's go!"

As she began to pedal and I followed suit, the pedal boat moved away from the dock (where

Nanny Beam and her agents were attempting to blend in with the tourists) and into the middle of the lake.

"I thought this would be the best way to get some privacy," the Queen said, gesturing to the lake. "And I rarely get the chance to do things like this. It's rather a lovely treat."

"You're very good at pedaling, Your Majesty," I wheezed, trying to keep up with her pace.

The Queen looked completely serene. She hadn't even broken a sweat. She must do a lot of spinning classes at Buckingham Palace or something.

"Patricia ... sorry, your Nanny Beam, tells me that you're finding it hard to concentrate at school?" the Queen said breezily.

Brilliant. When other kids have school issues, they get snitched on to their parents. When I fall short, I get snitched on to the QUEEN.

This superhero business isn't easy.

"It's difficult knowing Mr. Mercury still hasn't been found," I reasoned.

She stopped pedaling, so that we could just bob in the middle of the lake for a bit.

"Yes, I know what you mean. I've been finding it difficult to concentrate on anything else, too. We have to trust Nanny Beam and her team to track down Mr. Mercury and the Jewel of Truth and Nobility."

As she said the last bit, a shadow fell across her face. She looked tired and sad.

Only a handful of people in the world know that the octagonal St. Edward's Sapphire set in the diamond cross at the top of the Imperial State Crown isn't just any sapphire. According to legend there are four precious stones in existence, each with their own powers: the Light of the World, the Jewel of Truth and Nobility, the Gem of Wisdom and Peace, and the Heart of Love.

The sapphire in the Imperial State Crown is the Jewel of Truth and Nobility. The Queen is its guardian, just like every monarch of Britain has been throughout history. Just like I'm the guardian of the Light of the World.

The Queen and Nanny Beam had told me this HUGE secret, just before Mr. Mercury had stolen the crown from Buckingham Palace. They had thought that only they knew the true identity of the stone. But Darek had learned of its existence from his father before he died.

"We're going to get the Jewel of Truth and Nobility back, Your Majesty," I said determinedly. "Back with you, where it belongs."

She gave me a warm smile. "I have no doubt. I can't believe Mr. Mercury was under my nose that whole time. I feel so silly."

"We have all been fooled by Mr. Mercury," I assured her, remembering when he had been in disguise as sweet, bumbling personal assistant David Donnelly at the Superhero Conference, and I hadn't had a clue.

"What I want to know is why Mr. Mercury stole the crown when Darek was already in prison by then. Whose orders was he acting on and does he know how precious the stone really is?" She let out a long sigh. "Nanny Beam and I discuss it a lot. Darek must have planted

Mr. Mercury at the palace to steal the precious stone for him, while he focused on extracting the powers from the Light of the World. And then, when Darek was arrested and their plan was foiled, did Mr. Mercury decide to carry on with the scheme for himself? Or is he planning on selling the crown to the highest bidder?"

"Do you think Darek told him about the Jewel of Truth and Nobility, Your Majesty?"

"Perhaps. Or maybe he worked out that it must be important, for Darek to risk so much to gain it. Darek isn't saying a word." She shook her head before looking up at me with a hopeful smile. "At least the Light of the World is safe."

"Mum has hidden it until we can return it to where it belongs," I assured her. "Apparently it's somewhere no one would think to look and it has a good alarm system. I have no idea, but I'm guessing one of Nanny Beam's secret underground lairs."

"And when you say you'll return the Light of the World to where it belongs. . ."

I'll never forget the day Mum told me the Beam family legend, the same day I found out I had superpowers. Centuries ago, when the world was thrown into darkness, one of our ancestors, a young woman named Dawn, set off on a journey north to the aurora borealis, the northern lights. She discovered a precious stone there, returned light to the world and gained its powers. Every Beam woman since Dawn has been given the powers of light to help the world.

It was time the Light of the World should be returned to where it all began, where it would be safe: underneath the aurora borealis. I just had to find out exactly where in the frozen north my ancestor Dawn had discovered it.

"When the Jewel of Truth and Nobility is back safe with us, I'll return the Light of the World," I explained, admiring a swan as it elegantly drifted past us. "I'm going to do everything I can to help Nanny Beam track down Mr. Mercury. I won't let him win."

The Queen gave me a knowing smile and reached into the handbag that was on her lap. She pulled out a familiar book. It was the book about precious stones that I had ... ahem ... *borrowed* from the Natural History Museum. It contained all the old legends and folklore about them. It was thanks to this book that I had come to learn that the Light of the World wasn't the only precious stone with powers in existence.

"Here, take this," she said, passing the book to me. "Nanny Beam rescued it from Darek when he was arrested and loaned it to me to read. Various MI5 agents and scholars have been through it looking for clues as to what Darek had been planning to do next if he'd succeeded in extracting the powers from the Light of the World. They hoped that might help them work out what Mr. Mercury's plans may be."

"They didn't find anything?"

She shook her head. "Nothing. That's why I'm giving it to you. I want you to have another look at it. You and your friends, the Bright Sparks, have always been good at thinking outside the box. Maybe you'll see something they missed."

"Of course," I said, clutching the book tightly. "Although it will be difficult to ask the Bright Sparks to help when they don't know what the sapphire really is. They think it's terrible that Mr. Mercury has stolen the crown, but they have no idea what's at stake."

I hated lying to the Bright Sparks, but it

was the best way to protect them. After Mr. Mercury took the crown, Nanny Beam and I talked about whether we should reveal the truth about the precious stones to them, but we realized that telling them how important the stones really are would put all of them in great danger. And I couldn't do that to my friends. I couldn't risk them being a part of something so dangerous. The fewer people who know, the fewer Mr. Mercury can get to.

There was only one person we decided needed to know the whole truth: Mum.

Nanny Beam and I went for dinner with her one evening after Christmas and told her everything. It took her a while to get her head around it all, but I'm glad we told her. It makes me feel a little less alone in all of this.

"Yes, it is difficult hiding something so important from your close friends." The Queen nodded thoughtfully. "I know how you feel.

But at least we have each other and Nanny Beam."

"That's true."

I smiled up at her and we sat in silence for a moment, bobbing peacefully in the middle of the lake.

"I suppose we had better start pedaling back," the Queen said eventually. "Your grandmother will want to get you home before dark."

"Thanks for the book. And for taking the time to talk with me, Your Majesty. I really appreciate it."

"Thank *you* for all your help," she said, her eyes twinkling at me as she started to pedal back toward shore. "Lightning Girl, the world needs you once again."

As soon as I walked through the door, Kimmy jumped up and sent me flying backward.

"Hey, Kimmy!" I giggled. "I missed you, too!"

I couldn't stop laughing as my German shepherd pinned me to the ground with her big paws and covered my face in slobbery licks. My whole family is convinced that dogs can truly sense when something is up because Kimmy has been much more protective of me ever since I found out I had superpowers. When

I'm home, she barely leaves my side and she's even started creeping up to my bedroom in the night, opening the door – which she has recently worked out how to do (Kizzy told me German shepherds are superintelligent) – and settling down to sleep curled up at the side of my bed.

At first, when he learned of this new habit of hers, Dad kept trying to "lay down some ground rules" and told me that when I heard her come into the bedroom, I was to tell her no and take her back downstairs to her bed. But the two times that I did that, she just came right back up again, so we gave up. I'm secretly happy that she insisted on her new bedtime routine. I like knowing she's right there, beside me.

"I thought that commotion must be you arriving home," Mum said, coming into the hallway and smiling when she saw Kimmy standing over me. "Kimmy's been going to look out of the window for your return every five minutes."

"She's my protector, aren't you, Kimmy?"

Kimmy barked happily and gave me another slobbery lick.

"Come and get some food; you must be hungry after today. Unless you ate with Nanny Beam?"

"Nope, I'm starving," I said, scrambling to my feet. "I'll just be one minute."

As Mum went back to the others, I ran upstairs, Kimmy at my heels, and tucked the precious-stones book safely under my pillow. If Dad knew I had it, he might want it back, considering it technically belonged to him and the Natural History Museum. He was a professor of mineralogy there and had kept it in his office for research purposes. I would give it back to him eventually, but not yet.

I shut my bedroom door and headed back downstairs to the kitchen.

"Our big fashion star is home!" Mum announced, putting an arm round me and squeezing me close as I came through the door.

"Aurora!" Dad beamed, coming over to give me a big hug. "I am so proud of you! You were wonderful up there."

"Well done for not falling over flat on your face." Alexis grinned from the table, digging into what I imagined was at least his second helping of vegetable lasagna.

"Did Georgie really design this herself?" Clara asked, so mesmerized by the sequins on my jacket that she reached out to touch the sleeve and lost the page of the book she was reading. "It's very glamorous."

"Want to try it on?"

I shrugged the Lightning Girl jacket off and draped it over Clara's shoulders. She walked around the kitchen, swishing it about and making us all laugh. The sequins kept catching the light and Kimmy began chasing the resulting funny dots that appeared every now and then on the walls and floor.

"You know, wearing something like this makes me think that Coco Chanel really had a point when she said 'Fashion has to do with ideas, the way we live, what is happening,'" Clara quoted thoughtfully. "This jacket isn't just a jacket. It really means something. I might write a paper on that theory when I find a free moment. It would be interesting to branch away from science and get an insight into the world of fashion."

"Always good to try something new," Dad agreed, smiling warmly at her.

"Clara, does it ever occur to you that you're eight years old?" Alexis laughed, ruffling her hair, much to her annoyance. "When you have a free moment, you should be, I don't know" – he hesitated – "playing computer games or something."

Clara rolled her eyes. "How tempting, but I think I'll leave the gaming to you."

Alexis grinned and went back to his food. I had to admit that my brother and sister were dauntingly high achieving. Alexis was this big technology nerd who seemed to be able to hack or program anything. He spent most of his time at his computer and I've never seen him happier than when he was offered an internship at Vermore Enterprises, having discovered he was related to THE Darek Vermore, his icon.

Obviously, that was before any of us knew

that Darek Vermore was a bad guy trying to steal my powers.

Alexis doesn't like talking about what happened on the rooftop that day. When Darek comes up in conversation, Alexis's expression darkens, and he looks very angry and sad at the same time. It wasn't his fault at all, but he blamed himself for telling Darek Vermore what I had discovered in the book – that transferring the powers of the Light of the World was possible, but you needed the guardian to be present.

Darek had convinced Alexis he wanted the information for good reasons, and why shouldn't Alexis have believed him? Darek was working with Nanny Beam and MI5. He was on our side – a relation of the Beams who was looking out for his family after finally being reunited with them.

I must have told Alexis that a *hundred* times

over Christmas, but he wouldn't listen. He kept shaking his head and saying that he put his little sister in danger, something he couldn't forgive himself for. I told him that I could handle myself, but he said that as my big brother, it was his job to worry.

And, he added, to tease me for being a loser all the time.

"So, where were you after the show, Lightning Girl?" Alexis asked as Dad put a plate of heated-up food in front of me on the kitchen table.

Kimmy immediately came rushing over to sit next to me in case I needed any help eating it.

"I had a meeting with Nanny Beam," I explained. "And the Queen."

"The *Queen*?" Alexis blinked. "Are you serious?"

Mum and Dad came to sit down at the table

with us, Mum giving me a knowing look as she pulled in her chair.

"Yeah," I said, taking a sip of water, reminding myself to be careful with how much I gave away. "She wanted to talk about Mr. Mercury taking off with the crown after our ceremony. She thought I might be able to help track him down."

"Are you going to help MI5?" Clara asked.

Dad sighed. Last term, when we didn't know who the evil mastermind behind everything was, I had been determined to track down Mr. Mercury's whereabouts, knowing that it was the best link to finding out who he was working for. My enthusiasm for the mission got me into a lot of trouble.

I got ever-so-slightly arrested.

So, I couldn't imagine my parents were going to be happy with me going after a dangerous criminal once again.

"Actually, we've been discussing things," Mum began, looking at Dad, who gave her an encouraging nod. "We want to be honest with you three."

She took a deep breath.

"We wanted to let you know that after the events of last term, we're not going to hold you back from aiding Nanny Beam and MI5 to track down Mr. Mercury. Aurora" – she reached for my hand across the table – "if it wasn't for you and the Bright Sparks, something might have happened to Alexis without us even knowing. You deserved that medal the Queen gave you, and we don't want to stop you from doing what you do best." She grinned. "Saving the world."

I put my fork down and stared at her. "So . . . you're saying that you give me permission to do everything I can to track down Mr. Mercury?"

"Yes." Dad nodded. "But this time, you keep us informed. We know you're not going to stop until you find Mr. Mercury, whether you have our permission or not. This way, at least you can keep us in the loop. We won't be cross. We won't try to stop you. We want to know where you are and be able to help you wherever possible."

"This time round, we're going to work together," Mum added. "Deal?"

"Sounds good to me! Deal."

Dad beamed at me and Mum gave me a small smile when he wasn't looking. Mum knew about the precious stone set into the Queen's crown and how extra important it was to find Mr. Mercury this time; she wasn't going to try to stop me from helping.

"Right, how about we go set up a movie?" Dad said, clapping his hands together. "I think Aurora should choose after her amazing performance in the fashion show today."

"Seriously?" Alexis groaned. "But she has

the worst taste in films."

"Alexis," Dad said in a warning tone, "please help Aurora set it up while we clear the table."

Following Alexis into the sitting room, I was pleased to have a moment to speak to him alone. He picked up the remote and slumped onto the sofa. I sat down next to him, Kimmy hopping up next to me and resting her head in my lap.

"Alexis, can you do me a favor?" I asked.

"What's up?" Alexis yawned.

"Can you still get into the Vermore system?"

He looked at me in surprise. "I don't know. Why?"

"I had an idea on the way back from my meeting with the Queen," I explained. "Mr. Mercury might not be the only employee loyal to Darek. What if someone else at Vermore Enterprises is still helping Mr. Mercury, even though Darek is in prison? They might be in on whatever plan Darek had for the crown, too."

"It's a possibility," Alexis said thoughtfully. "When I interned there, everyone seemed very nice and not exactly the kind of people who would be involved in a royal heist, but I guess I thought Darek was really nice, too."

"I just wondered, if you could get into the Vermore computer system, you might come across something suspicious. Mr. Mercury may have contacted someone there or be using their technology somehow."

"Let me see what I can do," he said determinedly. "Their system will be hard to crack, but I'll find a way."

"Thanks, Alexis. You're the best."

"Anything I can do to make up for the mistakes I made last year," he said, returning to the TV. "Now, what does a superhero like watching on a Friday night?"

I was just about to read out some options when the doorbell rang. Dad came bustling through from the kitchen.

"Aurora, did you invite the Bright Sparks over?"

"No," I called from the sitting room. "Maybe Nanny Beam forgot to tell me something earlier and she's come back."

We heard him open the door and a familiar voice came floating through the house.

"My, Henry, you look tired," we heard Aunt Lucinda say. "Remind me to lend you my new moisturizer! The most expensive in the world, but so worth it, darling; it will get rid of those bags under your eyes. Honestly, you look twice your age!"

"Kiyana," Dad called to Mum in a VERY strained voice, "your sister and her pet ostrich are here. With a LOT of suitcases."

"Oh yes, didn't I mention that already? Alfred and I are here to stay with you for a few weeks! Won't this be FUN?"

"I've never heard an ostrich snore before," Fred said with a grimace.

The Bright Sparks had come over for a movie on Sunday afternoon, but we were having trouble hearing the film over Alfred's foghorn snores. We had excitedly walked into the sitting room, laden with popcorn and snacks, to find Alfred, in a white bathrobe, matching slippers and a towel wrapped in a turban around his head, sprawled across the entire sofa, fast asleep.

Aunt Lucinda, who came through from the

kitchen dressed in the same outfit and sipping a mocktail, explained that they had "just come from a luxury London spa. That's why Alfred's feathers are particularly fluffy today." She had then swanned past my friends to lie across the other sofa, before placing cucumber slices over her eyes and telling us to "carry on as usual," promising they wouldn't get in our way.

The only problem was we couldn't exactly carry on as normal as, thanks to them, there was nowhere to sit but the floor. And a few minutes into the film, Fred made the decision to turn it off since we couldn't hear any of it anyway.

"I didn't even realize ostriches *could* snore," Georgie said, watching Alfred with interest.

"Oh, he's a marvelous snorer," Aunt Lucinda commented without removing the cucumber slices from her eyes. "He won the International Snoring Championships two years in a row. I find his snores rather soothing. Don't you?"

The Bright Sparks didn't look convinced.

Aunt Lucinda had only been living here two days and already there had been plenty of chaos. Even though they are twins, Aunt Lucinda and my mum are very different. While Mum has dedicated her life to saving the world with her superpowers, Aunt Lucinda decided to spend her life using her superpowers to get whatever she wants. Aunt Lucinda is a lot of fun – she always wears bright colors and over-the-top statement outfits. And she doesn't go anywhere without her sidekick, Alfred, a grumpy ostrich who shares Aunt Lucinda's fondness for stealing expensive jewelry, conning their way into exclusive events and spending almost the whole year on luxury vacations.

In the first few hours, we discovered they weren't exactly ideal housemates. Ostriches are big creatures and Alfred was continually knocking everything over as he walked past. One of his favorite pastimes also happened to be destroying things. The moment he arrived, I hid my clothes under my bed, aware that he loved to "borrow" items of clothing and then rip them apart once he was done wearing them. He kept stealing the TV remote and insisting on watching soaps – "he just ADORES the dramatic story lines," Aunt Lucinda kept saying fondly – and then when Alexis couldn't take it anymore and attempted to remove the remote from him, Alfred swallowed it in protest.

Alexis almost passed out on the spot when he saw that Alfred had been into his room and stamped on his computer keyboard in frustration when he couldn't remember his email password, before pecking at the screen until it cracked.

Clara had found that quite funny until she realized that her room hadn't been left untouched either. Alfred had invented a game of tearing all the pages out of her science books and throwing them up in the air like confetti, so they would rain round him as he danced about the room happily. He'd then used permanent marker to draw some kind of weird blob with a beak in the middle of the whiteboard that she used to solve mathematical equations.

"Alfred did a self-portrait!" Aunt Lucinda said, her eyes welling up as she admired the board. "He is so talented."

Clara was so horrified, she couldn't speak for about half an hour.

And Aunt Lucinda had taken over the house with all her stuff. She had so many clothes that she insisted on hanging up everywhere because the closet in the spare room was "simply not big enough." Every door frame and curtain rail in the house was being used to hang up her clothes, so to get into a room you had to hack your way through a wall of ball gowns and poufy skirts.

"Mum, WHEN are they leaving?" Alexis asked almost every hour, but the answer was always the same.

They were here until Nanny Beam said so. She'd asked Aunt Lucinda and Alfred to stay at our house for a bit until Mr. Mercury had been found and put in prison.

"But we already have two superheroes in the house," Mum said to Nanny Beam in a VERY strained voice. "It's not like Lucinda and Alfred would be any help if Mr. Mercury did decide to pay us a visit!"

Nanny Beam disagreed, calmly reminding Mum of the times that Aunt Lucinda and Alfred had helped us out of scrapes in the past. She had a point. It had been my aunt and her ostrich who had rescued me when I was put under room arrest at the Superhero Conference, after being falsely accused of stealing the Light of the World. They had also come with the Bright Sparks to help Alexis and me stop Darek Vermore's scheme on the Vermore Enterprises rooftop before Christmas.

It was common knowledge that Alfred was now Mr. Mercury's great nemesis and vice versa. Without Alfred, things would have been much worse than they are now.

We just had to keep reminding ourselves of that.

"The film looked bad anyway. It's much nicer to be able to sit around and chat," Kizzy said cheerily, taking a handful of popcorn and pretending her hair wasn't flying around, getting more and more tangled every time Alfred exhaled.

I smiled at her. She really was the most optimistic and kindest person I'd ever met.

I was just about to tell her so when my phone sitting on the coffee table started ringing. Suzie glanced at the screen as she reached for it to pass it to me and her face lit up when she saw who it was.

"It's a video call with JJ and Cherry!"

The others all quickly huddled around me as I answered. The screen split into two as both Cherry and JJ's faces popped into view.

"Hi, everyone!" Cherry exclaimed, waving at her camera. "That was good timing. I thought JJ might be about and it looks like we caught all the Bright Sparks together!"

"Well, you two are honorary members," Suzie told her proudly.

JJ laughed. "If only we lived in the same country!"

I met JJ and Cherry at the Superhero Conference last summer. They both had superpowers, too – JJ was incredibly strong and fast; Cherry had supersonic hearing and had premonitions when something bad was going to happen. It was nice to meet others my age

with superpowers, so I didn't feel like such a freak. And then, when everyone thought I had stolen the Light of the World, Cherry and JJ helped me escape.

They all got along so well with the Bright Sparks, we'd ended up spending a week in Cornwall at Nanny Beam's together for some downtime after that particular adventure.

The only problem was that Cherry lived in Malaysia and JJ was from Nigeria. We could video call every now and then, but I still missed them a lot.

"How was the fashion show, Georgie?" Cherry asked, stifling a yawn. It may have been our afternoon, but it was late in the evening in Malaysia.

"It was good, thank you," Georgie said, blushing.

"That's an understatement," Suzie said, nudging Georgie. "It went viral! Everyone was talking about it and she got work experience offers from big fashion houses."

"That's amazing! Not that I'm surprised," Cherry said, causing Georgie to turn bright red.

"I saw it on YouTube," JJ said. "Nice going with the light beams, Aurora. Your jacket was amazing. Any chance you can design one for me, Georgie? Can it be leather with 'JJ' on the back? And maybe 'I am superstrong' down the sleeve?"

"Very creative," Cherry said, rolling her eyes. "Maybe we should leave the design to the designer. Anyway, I wondered if there was any news on the crown and Mr. Mercury. Has Nanny Beam gotten any new clues?"

"None so far."

"Don't worry, something will come up. And then you can... Hang on" – JJ paused, squinting into the screen – "is that a bunch of feathers behind you? And what's that loud noise every few seconds? It sounds like. . ."

"A bird with a sinus problem," Fred muttered, finishing his sentence.

"Please do not refer to Alfred as 'a bird,'" Aunt Lucinda said, lifting a cucumber slice to peer at Fred. "He gets very upset at being labeled as such."

"I don't think he'll have heard over his snores," Kizzy pointed out.

"I'm surprised you can't hear them from Malaysia, Cherry, with your supersonic hearing," Suzie said, making her giggle. "Put on your specially made headphones and see if you can tune in on them."

"So, Aunt Lucinda and Alfred are there?" Cherry asked, looking closer at the screen. "How come?"

"They've moved in for a bit," I explained through gritted teeth. "I'll tell you about it later."

"Hello, darlings!" Aunt Lucinda trilled from

her sofa. "I hope you're causing as much trouble as possible in your various corners of the globe."

"As always, Aunt Lucinda," JJ said proudly. "I'm currently grounded for practicing my karate chop on the kitchen table. Broke it clean in half."

"Marvelous. I shall report that back to Nanny Beam. She'll be thrilled to hear of your skills."

"So, no updates at all on finding Mr. Mercury?" Cherry said, bringing the conversation back on track.

I shook my head. "No leads as yet, but maybe something will come up soon."

"Has Nanny Beam spoken to Darek?" she asked suddenly.

"Probably," I said, glancing at Aunt Lucinda, who had decided to sit up and listen to the conversation. "He would have gone through lots of questioning before he was put in prison."

"Did she get anything out of him?"

"No," Aunt Lucinda replied for me. "He's hardly saying a word and he's told her nothing of interest."

"Have you been to talk to him, Aurora?"

"No," I said, confused. "Why? Do you think I should?"

"Maybe. I'm surprised you haven't already. Surely he's the best clue you can get?" Cherry reasoned. "Mr. Mercury was working for him, right?"

"Maybe he still is," JJ said enthusiastically.

"Of course, he's the best clue, but we've tried everything to get information out of him and nothing has worked. Nanny Beam has brought in experts and trained professionals from around the country," Aunt Lucinda said, picking a bit of fluff off her bathrobe. "He isn't giving us anything on Mr. Mercury."

"And if MI5 agents can't get anything out of him, then I doubt I'd have any success," I pointed out.

Cherry shrugged. "It was just an idea. If anyone knows where Mr. Mercury is, it's Darek Vermore."

There was silence for a few moments as we pondered Cherry's suggestion.

"I'm not sure Aurora would be allowed to go along and speak to him in the high-security prison without being accompanied," Aunt Lucinda noted. "She's ... well ... too young and not trained in these things."

"Maybe those are the very reasons it might just work," JJ said thoughtfully.

"Maybe," I said, the idea growing on me. "Or it could be completely hopeless."

"How will you know," Cherry said, leaning forward and smiling into the camera, "if you don't try?"

"Let me get this straight," Alexis said, sitting on the edge of my bed. "You're going to visit Darek Vermore . . . in *prison*?"

I nodded. "Nanny Beam has approved the plan and Aunt Lucinda is going to drive me there in a minute."

"Are you sure this is a good idea? Why would you want to see him again? And surely Nanny Beam has tried speaking to him. If she can't get any information from him. . ."

"I have to try," I said firmly.

I sat down next to him on the bed to tie the laces on my Lightning Girl sneakers. I felt like I needed all the confidence I could get today and somehow Georgie's designs always give me a little boost.

"You know what, Aurora, I realize I tease you a lot for being a loser and stuff," Alexis said, putting his hand on my shoulder, "but you truly are one of the bravest people I know."

I looked up from my shoes to see him beaming at me.

"You're not being sarcastic right now?" I asked suspiciously.

"Nope." He laughed. "I mean it."

"Oh." I smiled. "Thanks, Alexis. That's really nice of you to say. And . . . likewise."

"Just be careful," he warned as I turned back to my laces. "Remember how manipulative and intelligent Darek Vermore is. He managed to fool an entire government security service. Make sure you're on your guard."

"I will be. Don't worry."

He nodded. "Before you go, I wanted to tell you about something weird I discovered when I was taking a look around Vermore Enterprises's system."

"You managed to get into it?" I asked excitedly.

"Of course." He shrugged like it was no big deal that he'd hacked into the computer system of one of the largest tech giants in the world. "I think with their boss in prison and all the scandal surrounding Darek, the people at Vermore have let their guard down a bit. Anyway, it took me a while, but I managed it."

"Did you find any trace of Mr. Mercury?"

"No, nothing like that, but" – he added hurriedly, noticing my disappointment – "I did find something strange. On the day of the showdown on Vermore Enterprise's rooftop — the day Darek Vermore revealed that he had the Light of the World and was going to steal your powers — he arranged a private flight to Iceland."

I blinked at him. "A flight to . . . Iceland?"

"Yeah, weird, right?" Alexis raised his eyebrows. "But the weirdest thing about it is the *time* that he made the arrangements. I checked out the time stamp of the booking on his account, and it looks like he got in contact with the pilot, just after he'd kidnapped me and left me tied up on the roof with his security team. Seriously, from the looks of it, he must have arranged the flight as he was making his way down the stairs from the rooftop door and toward the elevator. Don't you think that's strange?"

I nodded slowly, my brain utterly confused by this new information.

"Why would he arrange a trip to Iceland when he thought he'd finally gotten the key to transferring the powers of the Light of the World to himself?" Alexis asked, his brow furrowed in concentration. "He was just about to become the most powerful person on the planet. Why book a last-minute vacation to Iceland? It doesn't make any sense. And why book it in secret?"

"What do you mean?"

"I spoke to his assistant this morning and he didn't know anything about it," Alexis explained. "I don't think he's lying either; he seems very upset that he's been working all this time for an evil genius trying to take over the world. Anyway, it may mean absolutely nothing. Maybe he thought he'd want a little break after transferring the powers and booked a weekend break on a whim. But I thought you should know. You can bring it up when you see him later."

"Thanks, Alexis."

"Aurora?" Aunt Lucinda called up the stairs. "Are you ready to go?"

"Coming!" I yelled back, standing up and turning to Alexis. "I'll see you in a bit."

"See you in a bit, Lightning Girl," he said. "And be careful."

*

As I stood looking up at the towering gates and walls of the high-security prison, I wondered whether it had been such a good idea asking Aunt Lucinda and Alfred to wait in the car. I was determined to do this on my own because I needed to be able to speak to Darek Vermore freely about the stones. But I suddenly didn't feel so confident anymore.

I didn't have the Bright Sparks by my side, either. When I told them I really was going to see Darek in prison, they offered to come with me, but I told them I was fine doing it on my own. As far as they were concerned, the Light of the World was safe and, although it was important to get the Imperial State Crown back to the Queen and bring Mr. Mercury to justice, it wasn't like the world was in grave danger. They didn't know how precious that crown was and what it contained.

"We just need you to sign in here," the prison guard said to me when I came in, sliding me a folder from behind his glass screen.

I took the folder and filled in my name and details, including who I was visiting, at the bottom of the front form, underneath a list of previous prison visitors. I was just about to hand it back when something caught my eye. An entry from a few days before.

A visitor for Darek Vermore who had signed themselves in as "N."

"Everything all right?" the prison officer asked, wondering why I was just staring at the list.

"Yeah... It's just ... do you remember this visitor?" I pointed at the entry.

He shook his head. "No, sorry. I wasn't on duty then."

"No worries," I said, passing back the folder. "I'm ready to go through now."

He nodded and waved over another prison officer to escort me. Loud buzzers went off over our heads as each door was opened to let us through to the next part of the corridor. I followed the officer nervously, wondering who that visitor could possibly be. Was it Mr. Mercury in disguise? Would he really risk coming to visit Darek in prison?

"Here we are," the officer said, stopping at a door. "We have instructions from Patricia Beam of the British Security Service to let you speak to the prisoner privately?"

"Yes." I gulped. "That's right."

"I'll be just out here," he said warily.

"Are you sure you don't want someone with you? It doesn't seem right... You should be accompanied by—"

"Trust me, it's OK," I said, pointing to my sneakers. "I can handle this."

He smiled knowingly. "I thought it was you. I'm a big fan, Lightning Girl. Well, the minute you feel uncomfortable, you just call out and I'll come in."

"Thank you."

He opened the door and held it for me. I stepped through to see Darek Vermore sitting at a lone table in the middle of a windowless room, his wrists in thick metal handcuffs attached to the table. The first thing I noticed was how odd it was to see him in anything other than a sharp, tailored suit. He looked so different in the dull-gray prison uniform. And he looked tired. Very tired.

I had to be calm to get him to talk to me,

but just seeing him, the anger bubbled up inside me as I thought about everything he had tried to do and what he had put my family through.

"Aurora," he said quietly as I came to sit on the chair opposite him. "What are you doing here?"

"I'm here to speak to you," I said, my hands feeling very clammy as they gripped the sides of the chair. "I wanted to ask you some questions."

He watched me carefully. "Nanny Beam is trying a different tactic, then? Sending in *you* to get some answers. I'm not going to tell you anything."

"Has Mr. Mercury visited you in prison?" I blurted out, the visitors' book still on my mind.

A smile crossed his lips. "Do you think he would be that silly?"

"Then who came to see you this week? I saw the logbook."

He leaned forward to rest his forearms on the table and clasp his hands together, before bringing his eyes up to look up at me earnestly.

"I'm sorry, Aurora. For everything."

I stared at him.

"I'm sorry for everything I did," he

continued. "I never should have turned against you and your family." He let out a long sigh and shook his head. "I was consumed by jealousy and getting revenge for my father's death. Prison has given me plenty of time to think. You have no idea what it's like in here."

"If you think I'm going to believe a word you say—"

"I think we can help each other," he said suddenly.

"What? Look, Darek, I'm here because I have to track down Mr. Mercury. Does he know about the Jewel of Truth and Nobility?"

Darek pursed his lips, refusing to answer.

"You know as well as I do what's at stake," I continued. "I know you don't want to tell us anything because you hate the Beam family, but think about this — that precious stone in the hands of *Mr. Mercury*. Whether he knows what it is now because you told him, or whether he discovers what it truly is, do you really want *him* to have it?"

He looked at me curiously. Last night, I had barely slept, my mind racing with ideas and angles that I could use to try to get information from him. This was the best one I'd thought of.

"Do you think that he's going to help you?" I continued. "He doesn't need you anymore. He's got something incredibly powerful in his possession. If you help us track him down and return the crown, maybe Nanny Beam will be able to help you."

He nodded slowly.

"I don't want the stone in the hands of that oaf, it's true. And I don't want to spend my life locked in here. I miss the comforts. The vacations. The luxuries. I was one of the richest people in the world and now" – he gestured around him with a dismal expression – "I have nothing. And do you know what the worst thing is? I don't have a family."

"You never wanted a family," I reminded him, narrowing my eyes. "Nanny Beam was your family; we were your family, and you betrayed us. Alexis worshipped you."

"I know," he said, waving his hand for me to stop with a very convincing pained expression. "I regret it all."

"I'm not an idiot, Darek," I said, crossing my arms. "So, you can stop acting as though you're actually sorry and instead start helping me to track down Mr. Mercury."

"Aurora, please, I want to help you," he said desperately. "But the information I can give you is all I have left."

"What do you mean?"

"I have nothing now but my knowledge. It's the one bargaining chip I can use to get out of here." He took a deep breath. "Aurora, I will tell you where Mr. Mercury is."

"You will?" I leaned forward eagerly. I couldn't believe I'd done it.

He held up his hand. "If you get me out of prison."

"WHAT?" I looked at him like he was mad. "Is that a joke?"

"I can't give you his whereabouts for nothing in return. I want to help you; I want to give you answers. I can take you to Mr. Mercury. But you must help me to get out of here. Those are my terms."

"Never."

"Then you'll never find the crown and the precious stone that is set within it." He shrugged. "It's up to you. I'm not offering this deal to anyone else, not even Nanny Beam."

"Why not?"

"Because I don't trust any of them not to go back on their word. I really am sorry, and I want to make up for what I did. I want to help you catch Mr. Mercury and keep the precious stone safe."

I shook my head at him and stood up abruptly, the chair legs screeching across the floor. The prison officer waiting outside immediately opened the door and stepped in to make sure everything was all right.

"I'm leaving," I said to Darek. "If you were truly sorry you'd help, even if there was nothing in it for you. You're going to be stuck in here a long time."

I turned on my heel and marched toward the guard waiting to escort me out.

"Think about my offer," I heard Darek call out just as the door shut behind me. "It's all in your hands now, Lightning Girl."

"I did NOT scream," Fred declared adamantly. "I had something stuck in my throat. It was a cough. Not a scream."

Suzie and Georgie shared a smile. We were on a school field trip to Warwick Castle and had just been on an immersive tour of the castle dungeon. When the guide had warned our group that the tour involved actors and was "scary and jumpy" before we went in, Fred had snorted and whispered to the rest of us Bright Sparks that he hardly thought "a

few dark stone rooms and people in costume"
counted as scary.

We emerged from the dungeons with Fred
looking mildly traumatized.

"Sounded like a scream to me when that
actor jumped out at you, Fred," Suzie said,
raising her eyebrows at him. "A high-pitched,
terrified scream."

"Like I said, it was a *cough*," Fred repeated
through gritted teeth. "Easy to get those
confused."

Georgie smiled. "Sure," she said. "And what
about when you begged Aurora to use her light
beams to light up the scary dungeon cells?"

"I don't know what you're talking about,"
Fred said breezily. "I may have *asked* Aurora if
she wanted to use her light beams if she was a
little nervous. . ."

"Yeah, sure, *Aurora* was the nervous one."
Suzie rolled her eyes. "I don't remember Aurora

hiding behind my back when they asked for a volunteer."

"I was NOT hiding," Fred protested, fiddling with his collar. "I just wanted to make sure everyone could see, and if I stood in front of you, you might not have been able to see as well."

"Come on," Kizzy said, reaching into her bag and pulling out a book. "Let's go explore the rest of the castle. This place has an amazing history. You know, Queen Elizabeth I visited the castle in 1572." Kizzy paused and looked down at her feet in wonder. "She may have stood on this exact stone that I'm standing on."

"Kizzy, is that a book on Warwick Castle?" I asked, noting the title on the spine.

"Yep, I borrowed it from the school library specially for the trip," she told us proudly, flicking it open to a bookmarked page. "If anyone has any questions, let me know."

"That may be the geekiest thing you've ever done, Kizzy," Suzie said.

"No, what about the time she brought the French culture encyclopedia to Paris? And then dragged it about with her every day to all the sights," Fred pointed out.

"Oh yeah." Suzie nodded. "That was pretty geeky."

"I don't remember any of you complaining when I used said encyclopedia to knock out one of Darek Vermore's henchmen," Kizzy said, her cheeks going pink.

Georgie giggled, throwing an arm round her. "Don't worry, we love you for your geekiness. The Bright Sparks wouldn't get anywhere without you and your books."

"Come on, let's go see the turrets," Suzie said, leading the way. "Apparently, the view is amazing from the top. Unless you'd find it too frightening, Fred?"

"Very funny," Fred grumbled. "For the last time, it was a COUGH."

As Suzie and Georgie continued to tease Fred on the spiral stone steps up to the top of the castle, Kizzy hung back slightly to fall into step with me.

"While we're on the topic of books, I've had a chance to go through that one the Queen gave you," she said, patting her bag. "I brought it along with me today because I think I found a couple of things in there that might interest you."

I stopped in the middle of the staircase.

"What is it?" I asked excitedly.

I had lent Kizzy the book after we'd finished chatting to JJ and Cherry on the video call. I had glanced through it already and not found anything helpful, so I decided to ask Kizzy to look over it, too.

"I'll show you when we get to the top," she

said, as we both started to get a little out of breath climbing all the stairs.

Suzie, being the sportiest girl in school, was way ahead of the rest of us and was already at the top, calling down for us to hurry up and see the view. By the time we got there, she and Fred were arguing over whether a small blob in the distance was a cow or a horse.

"Wow!" Georgie smiled, leaning forward on the wall and looking out at the beautiful countryside. "You can see for miles!"

Kizzy reached into her bag and pulled out the precious-stones book, riffing through it to a certain page and then passing it to me.

"You see?"

My eyes scanned the two pages in front of me. "What am I looking at?"

"Look closely."

She pointed to the top left-hand corner of the first page and then the top right-hand corner of the second page. I examined the page numbers printed in the corners and gasped, looking up to see her watching me with a satisfied expression.

"There's a page missing here," she said, as I looked again to make sure I wasn't seeing things. "The page numbers don't follow on correctly. But whoever took this page managed to rip it out so neatly that you can hardly tell. They did a very good job of hiding it."

"They really did," I whispered, running my finger down the middle of the pages to see if I could feel any sign of torn paper.

"It may not be important, but I thought I should let you know. I don't know what was on the page that was here."

"I do," I said quietly.

"What are you two talking about over here?" Suzie asked, coming to join us. "You've barely noticed the view. Are the facts in that book about Warwick Castle really that fascinating?"

"This isn't that book; this is the precious-stones one that we helped Aurora steal from the Natural History Museum last term, remember?" Kizzy explained. "Last night, I realized that there was a page missing. Someone's torn it out."

"Seriously?" Georgie peered over my shoulder at the book. "You think it has something to do with Mr. Mercury and Darek?"

"Maybe." Kizzy shrugged. "Or it could have already been torn out years ago before any of this happened. It is an old book."

"Your dad may have torn it out, Aurora," Suzie suggested.

Kizzy snorted. "No way. Professor Beam would never vandalize a book. Trust me."

"Alfred could have done it when he was in one of his moods and you weren't looking," Georgie said with a smile. "He is such a funny ostrich."

"No, this has something to do with Mr. Mercury and Darek," I stated firmly. "I know it."

"How?" Georgie asked, her brow furrowed.

"Because I know what was on the page that's meant to be here," I said, tapping the book. "It was the page that mentioned the Light of the World. Darek may have ripped it out after he kidnapped Alexis. But if Darek still had it, Nanny Beam would have found it on him on the rooftop or when MI5 swept his office. Someone else has it now and I would bet anything that it's in the hands of Mr. Mercury."

"But why would Mr. Mercury be interested in the legend of the Light of the World now? He doesn't have the stone itself," Suzie pointed out, prompting the others to nod in agreement. "Surely he's given up on that whole plan now."

"Yeah, and he doesn't have Darek's resources or his brains to come up with a new plan to steal the Light of the World again without Darek helping him out, which he can't do from prison," Kizzy added. "He's got the Imperial State Crown now and he'll just be interested in making as much money as possible from that." She let out a sigh and shook her head. "I can't believe the petty Blackout Burglar was once our *teacher*."

I pursed my lips, wishing I could tell them.

"Are you OK, Aurora?" Kizzy asked, noticing my pained expression.

"Yeah," I replied. "I just wish. . . I wish Darek had told me something useful when I went to visit him."

Georgie put a comforting hand on my shoulder. "The fact that you went to visit him at all is amazing. I don't think I would have been brave enough to go into prison and face him again."

"Aurora, there's another thing that I think is

important," Kizzy continued, turning the page and pointing at the top paragraph. "Did you read this bit?"

I shook my head. "I don't think so. I was always focusing on the page that's now missing as that had the passage about how to transfer the powers."

"Well, I think you should read this." Kizzy smiled. "You had a feeling that the safest place for the Light of the World would be under the aurora borealis, didn't you?"

I nodded. "Yeah, I just believe it belongs where it was found."

"You're right, at least according to this legend you are. It's only a small mention, but it sounds similar to what you're thinking." Kizzy brushed her finger along the sentences, reading aloud. "*One myth that has been mostly forgotten or ignored surrounds the most precious stone of all. Resting under the northern lights, the* stone protects the natural balance of light and dark in the world, and all those who live within this balance."

"How did I miss this?" I whispered, reading the passage again.

"It doesn't specify that it's talking about the Light of the World, so it may not have stood out to you," Kizzy reasoned.

"Hey!" Fred called, gesturing for us to join him as he looked out at the view. While we had been chatting for the past few minutes, he'd been pretending to be an archer at the watch of the castle turret. "You need to come and see this!"

"I told you, Fred," Suzie said, rolling her eyes, "it is definitely a horse."

"No, not that. Something else."

I slung my backpack over my shoulder, heavy now with the added weight of the book, and followed the other three to crowd round him and look out to where he was pointing.

"Whoa," Suzie said, her eyes widening. "That looks . . . creepy."

Far in the distance, the sky had turned black, even though it was the middle of the day, casting a dark shadow over the land beneath it. All the lights in the shops and offices beneath it flickered and then turned off completely.

"Is that a storm?" Georgie asked nervously. "I hope it's not coming our way. Maybe we should go inside the castle just in case."

"It's miles away," Fred said, peering at it with interest.

"Yeah, but Georgie's right, we should head in," Kizzy said. "Storms can move fast."

As they all moved away from the edge of the wall and headed back down the spiral stone steps, I stood looking out at the patch of black sky for a few moments longer. A shiver ran down my spine and my fingers began to tingle with my powers.

Georgie was wrong. That was not a normal storm. It was the sky over yet another part of the world growing darker.

THE DA

HOMES F
AS DA
ENGU

Special report by Henry Nib

Homes and offices in parts of London
have been evacuated due to the
growing phenomenon of dark skies and
power cuts. Residents and workers based in
the Belgravia and Westminster regions of
London have been moved by the Metropolit
Police due to safety concerns.

LY SCOPE

ACUATED
RKNESS
F'S LONDON

a press conference this morning, the ame Minister insisted that this shouldn't ause widespread panic: "There is no cause ...or alarm. On advice from the Metropolitan Police and the emergency services, evacuating the areas most affected by this unusual darkness is simply a precaution."

There have been unconfirmed reports that the Queen is remaining at her residence in Buckingham Palace, despite the palace sitting in what's considered the darkest spot in the capital at present.

7

When we drew up to an abandoned building, I turned to the MI5 agent sitting next to me.

"Are you sure this is the right place?"

"Yes."

I peered out of the car window. We were in East London and had driven along busy, buzzing roads to end up down an empty, narrow street. At the top stood an old, rundown house that looked like no one had been inside for decades. The windows were boarded up and covered in cool graffiti, and there was a thick chain looped through the door handles, secured with a big padlock.

"Are you *doubly* sure?" I asked the secret service agent.

She turned her head slowly to look at me through her sunglasses. "*Yes.*"

"Have you ever been wrong about stuff like this?"

The agent smiled. "No. That's why your grandmother hired me."

"Right." I nodded, biting my lip. "Because you guys are her best and most trusted agents. So, there's no way you'd take me to a haunted house that might be a trap."

"Exactly."

"And this is where Nanny Beam told you to bring me."

"This is the place." The agent leaned across me to open the car door. "After you."

As she and another agent led me toward

the building, I wondered why the Queen and Nanny Beam couldn't just hold their meetings at Buckingham Palace. What was with all these odd places? A crow squawked loudly from the roof of the building as we walked up to it, making me jump.

I gulped as it flew off. I think I preferred being on the pedal boat on the Serpentine.

"Over here," the female agent said, noticing I was lagging behind and gesturing for me to follow her down the side of the building where there was a big metal door with "KEEP OUT" written across it in blood-red paint. The paint had dripped down from the letters before drying, so it looked as though it was straight out of a horror movie.

"Just to confirm, this *definitely* isn't a haunted house, is it?" I squeaked. "Because I know this meeting is important, but I'm really not a fan of ghosts or anything that's going to eat me alive."

The corners of the agent's mouth twitched as she tried to suppress a smile, and for a moment she reminded me of someone, but I couldn't think who. She came to stand over me and spoke in a low voice so that the other agents couldn't hear.

"I promise, Lightning Girl, that like many things in life, this isn't what it looks like." She smiled gently. "It's not haunted. And even if it was haunted, you've got me to protect you."

I nodded. "Right. You're right. Thanks."

"Don't mention it." She straightened up and went to wrench open the door. "This way."

I timidly stepped through the door and followed her down the stairs and along a corridor, dimly lit by a couple of bare light bulbs dangling from the ceiling. I thought about using my powers to brighten the space up a bit, but I'd already embarrassed myself in front of the agents with the whole ghost comment and I didn't want them to think I was scared of the dark, too. I hoped this wasn't some weird superhero bravery test that Nanny Beam had decided to put me through because if it was, then I was going to fail.

"Here we are," the agent said as we reached the door at the end of the corridor. "Enjoy."

She pushed open the door. My eyes lit up at the incredible sight before me. It was a massive, sparkling new, underground bowling alley.

"What is this place?" I asked, gazing round me in awe.

"Aurora! You're here."

The Queen was sitting with Nanny Beam in a booth at the milkshake bar on one side of the room. She stood up and came over to greet me.

"Hello, Your Majesty," I said, curtsying.

As my eyes fell to the floor, I couldn't help but notice that the Queen was wearing personalized bowling shoes, which had corgis

and crowns all over them.

"What do you think?" the Queen said as Nanny Beam gave me a hug.

"It's amazing! Is this your personal bowling alley?"

"Sadly, no." She chuckled. "It is about to open to the public, once they spruce up the outside of the building a little. The owner happens to know my secret love of the sport and kindly invited me to try out the lanes before the grand opening."

"Get your shoes on and let's get to it," Nanny Beam said.

She nodded to one of the bowling alley staff who came scurrying over holding out some shoes in my size. He looked like he was about to pass out on the spot and couldn't stop staring at the Queen as though he didn't quite believe she was standing right there.

"Thank you, Jon." Nanny Beam smiled at him as he bowed his head awkwardly and shuffled back to stand in front of all the pigeonholes stuffed with bowling shoes, and stare at the Queen some more.

"Check this out, Aurora." The Queen grinned, holding up a purple bowling ball with gold swirly lettering across it which read:

Her Majesty the Queen's Royal Bowling Ball
HANDS OFF!

"That is so cool!"

"Isn't it?" she said, admiring it. "It was a birthday present from my grandchildren. Right then, Lightning Girl, let's see what you're made of."

As she headed to the first lane that had been set up for us, I sidled up to Nanny Beam and whispered in her ear.

"I thought we were having a meeting."

"We are," Nanny Beam assured me, ushering me toward the lane. "It's nice to make it a little more fun."

As Nanny Beam and I waited our turn, the Queen took her run-up and launched her royal bowling ball straight down the middle of the lane at great speed, smashing into the pins and sending them flying.

"Strike!" she cried, turning to the secret service agent who'd been so nice to me and giving her a high five.

"Well done, Your Majesty!" Nanny Beam grinned, giving her a round of applause. "Although I'm determined not to let you win . . . again."

"Am I awake?" I asked Jon, the staff member who had brought me a milkshake on a silver tray. "Is this actually happening?"

He looked at the Queen, who was now doing a celebratory moonwalk in her corgi bowling shoes. He turned back to me.

"I'm really not sure myself," he whispered.

"Aurora, you're up!" the Queen announced, pointing at my name flashing on the screen above her head.

After a few rounds, during which we established that I was useless at bowling, Nanny Beam was pretty good at bowling, and the

Queen was at a professional level of bowling, it was decided that we should take a break to discuss the matters at hand.

"Have you seen the new reports about parts of the world getting darker?" the Queen asked, as I nodded in response. "It's worrying. We're not sure what's causing it and it seems to be spreading, particularly over London. Any updates, Patricia?"

"I've got my best people working on it," Nanny Beam said determinedly.

"We need to get to the bottom of it. I don't want people to be afraid to leave their homes," the Queen said, her eyebrows knitted together in concern. "The more I think about it, the more I worry it's to do with the precious stones."

"I'm not sure if this is linked, but we noticed something in the book you lent me," I said, getting it out of my bag. "Well, Kizzy noticed it. Here" – I turned to the bookmarked page and held it open on my lap for them to see – "look at the page numbers. There's a page missing. It's an important one, too. The page all about the legends of the stones and their guardians, along with the beliefs of the ability to transfer their powers."

"My goodness," Nanny Beam said, peering at the book. "I can't believe we missed this. It's not possible."

"It's easy to miss," I pointed out. "They've done it so neatly."

"No. No, this can't..." Nanny Beam stared down at it with a troubled expression. "It can't have been torn out recently; this book has been in my possession at MI5 since the moment we arrested Darek."

"Do you think Mr. Mercury has the missing page?" the Queen asked as Nanny Beam continued to look perplexed.

"Yes," I replied. "I don't know how he got it from Darek before he was arrested, but I think the other two precious stones could be in danger. Mr. Mercury may not be able to get the Light of the World, but I have a strong feeling he'll be going after the other two now that he has the Jewel of Truth and Nobility." I took a deep breath before putting forward my next request. "I've been thinking about it and I'd like to visit the other precious-stone guardians and check that they're safe. Mr. Mercury may be an idiot, but he's a master of disguise. All three of us here have been victims of that. The other guardians need to be warned and we should double their security."

"Aurora," Nanny Beam said gently, "it's an important point and kind of you to offer, but the other guardians are safe, as are the stones in their charge. There was nothing in that book about who the guardians could be, so even if

Mr. Mercury is now aware of their existence, he won't know where to start. Only the Queen and I know that information."

"Darek found out about the Jewel of Truth and Nobility, and you didn't think he knew anything about it," I pointed out.

"That was different. His father knew and passed on that information to him."

"My point is, it *is* possible to find out," I emphasized. "I think it's important to remember that Darek devoted his entire life to finding the precious stones. He recognized the Light of the World before any of us knew what it was. Even the Beams. He knew I was the guardian before I did."

Nanny Beam and the Queen shared a look.

"What if he found out about the other precious stones?" I continued. "What if he had others helping him track them down? Mr. Mercury could have bugged the palace.

Darek could have bugged the offices of MI5 when he was working with you, Nanny Beam. What if he overheard a conversation between you two about the stones and where they are? All I'm saying is I think we should take every precaution and I don't think we should underestimate Darek's knowledge or Mr. Mercury's determination. For all we know, they may still be working together. I think it's important to personally check in with the guardians, whoever and wherever they are."

The Queen nodded slowly. "Let me think about it, Aurora."

An agent came forward and whispered something in her ear. She rolled her eyes and stood up.

"Excuse me for a moment, I'm needed on the phone."

As she followed the agent to take the call, Nanny Beam excused herself to use the bathroom. I slumped back against the chair and sipped my milkshake, hoping that they had taken what I'd said seriously. When you're twelve years old, it's sometimes difficult to get adults to listen to you, whether you have superpowers or not.

While they were gone, I checked my phone and saw two missed calls from Alexis as well as a text message from him saying: PICK UP, LOSER, IT'S URGENT.

I didn't hesitate to call him back, remembering last year in Paris when I ignored his calls and then it turned out he was calling me because he'd found out that Darek was a bad guy.

"Hey," he said, answering on the first ring. "Where have you been?"

I glanced round the bowling alley. "It's a long story. Everything OK?"

"Yeah, you're on speakerphone and Clara's here, too."

"Hi, Aurora," Clara said. "We think we've got something."

"Our little sister is absolutely brilliant," Alexis said, and I could hear that he was grinning. "I know you already knew that, but she is ESPECIALLY brilliant today."

"Go on."

"I have just been going through some police files Alexis hacked into; old records and burglaries of Mr. Mercury's—"

"Wait, Alexis, you hacked into police files?" I asked, keeping my voice down and checking over my shoulders that no agents were listening.

"Yeah, I thought it might come in handy," he explained. "Turns out I was right. Clara, tell her."

"As we all know, Mr. Mercury's calling card of his early burglaries was to plunge buildings into darkness and then he'd steal everything, hence how he got the nickname the Blackout Burglar."

"Right."

"But the thing is, Mr. Mercury doesn't *exist* before these burglaries, or before he got a position at the school. Just like Joe the Butler didn't exist before he got the position at Buckingham Palace, or David Donnelly at the Superhero Conference. Mr. Mercury made up these characters and gave them backgrounds."

"Okaaaay?"

"So, who was Mr. Mercury before all this?" Clara asked excitedly. "What's his real name? I thought, if I could find out who he really was, it might throw up more places that he could be."

"Aurora," Alexis jumped in, "she did it! She found out his real name!"

"WHAT?" I pressed the phone to my ear. "Are you serious?"

"I did some research and there was a school in Surrey that had a series of blackouts during the time when Mr. Mercury would have been the right age to be a pupil," Clara explained. "The headmaster at the time reported it to the police, but they couldn't find the culprit. Loads of stuff kept going missing during these blackouts, and, not only that, but on rare occasions any witnesses saw the thief, they all gave completely different descriptions. What are the chances of different thieves using the exact same technique in a school?"

"He was perfecting his technique," Alexis added. "Blackouts AND disguise."

"So, you definitely think it's him?" I asked.

"It's him all right," Alexis said. "Clara found an old school photograph. I'm sending it through to you now. Check out the class of 1990. Right at the end of the second row, to the left."

I checked my phone screen and tapped on his message. The image flashed up on my screen. I scanned my eyes along the second row to the end and I did a double take. My jaw fell to the floor. The likeness was uncanny.

"Have you seen it?" I heard Alexis say.

I quickly put the phone to my ear again.

"Oh my goodness," I croaked, my mouth suddenly very dry. "It's him. It's Mr. Mercury."

"Yep, his real name is Desmond Silicon," Clara stated. "And do you want to know the best news of all?"

"What?"

"He's still registered as living at his mum's house in Surrey. We have his address."

"This is it," I said, gesturing to the house in front of us.

Georgie, Suzie, Kizzy and Fred, who was holding Kimmy on her leash, all came to stand next to me in a line to stare up at the house. I hadn't planned on bringing Kimmy all the way to Surrey with us to track down this Mrs. Silicon, but when she saw me put on my Lightning Girl sneakers and pick up my bag she went berserk and barred my way to the front door. The only way I could get her to move was to pick up her leash, assuring her that wherever I was off to, she was coming, too.

"But, it looks . . . normal," Fred commented.

"Yeah," Georgie agreed. "Perfectly normal. Are you sure this is the right address?"

I nodded, checking it on my phone. "This is the address Alexis gave me."

"Do you really think Mr. Mercury lives here?" Suzie asked, admiring the perfectly arranged flower beds lining the edge of the front garden.

"There's only one way to find out," Kizzy answered, marching down the driveway to the front door. "Come on."

"What happens if he's in there?" Georgie said, glancing up at the windows. "What do we do?"

"I've told Nanny Beam we're following a lead," I assured her, holding up my phone. "If we see him, I'll call her straightaway and MI5 will be here within minutes. We can stall him until then."

We surrounded Kizzy as she pressed the doorbell and stood back as we heard footsteps. The door swung open. It was her. Mrs. Silicon. The resemblance was uncanny. It was as though Mr. Mercury had just shoved a wig on his head and put on some lipstick.

"Hello," she said brightly. "Can I help you?"

"Does ... does Mr. Silicon live here?" I asked timidly.

"Yes, he's my son."

I stared at her, hardly daring to believe that this was Mr. Mercury's mother. This was the biggest lead we could possibly have found.

"We're old students of his," Georgie said, jumping in to help me as my brain floundered. "We were in the area and we wanted to drop by and say hello."

Mrs. Silicon's face lit up and she placed her hands over her heart.

"Oh, how wonderful!" she exclaimed, standing aside to usher us past her and into the house. "Come in! Come in! What a pleasure to meet some of his students. You come in and make yourselves comfortable. And what a lovely dog! You're very welcome too, little darling. What's her name?"

"Kimmy."

"Hello, darling Kimmy."

She crouched down to give Kimmy a pat on the head and a scratch behind the ears. Kimmy wagged her tail and got that dopey expression on her face that she gets whenever she knows she's about to have a good fuss made of her. Mrs.

Silicon may have looked like Mr. Mercury, but she was so warm and genuine, it seemed strange that she was related to him.

She instructed us to make ourselves at home in the sitting room and went to put the kettle on. The house was lovely and cozy, and particularly neat. I sat down on the sofa and took in the room, trying to picture Mr. Mercury growing up here.

"What do we do?" Suzie whispered.

"Just keep asking questions about Mr. Mercury... I mean, Silicon," Kizzy instructed in a low voice. "We need to get as much information out of her as possible. She might give away a clue as to where he is."

"What if he's in this house *right now*?" Georgie said. "We'd have him cornered!"

The door opened and we all quickly sat back, pretending to be innocently looking around the room.

"Here you go, everyone, help yourselves," Mrs. Silicon said, bringing in a tray of tea mugs and some cookies. As we all reached for a mug, Mrs. Silicon handed everyone a cookie and snapped off a little bit of hers to give to Kimmy.

"Kimmy, sit!" Mrs. Silicon instructed in a firm voice.

Kimmy sat perfectly.

"Clever, clever girl," she cooed, giving her the cookie and then sitting down in the armchair, with Kimmy settling at her side.

I was amazed at how Mrs. Silicon had turned so authoritative and then all warm and smushy again when Kimmy had done what she was told. She reminded me of Nanny Beam a lot. Just without the bright-pink hair.

"So, is Mr. Silicon upstairs?" Kizzy asked, squished into the sofa next to me.

"He's away, I'm afraid," she answered, before

misinterpreting our collective disappointed expressions. "How lovely that you're so fond of him; I'm so sorry he's not here! I'm sure he would have been delighted to have seen you. He loves to talk about his teaching days."

"This is a nice room," Suzie commented, glancing around the shelves. "If you don't mind me asking, you don't seem to have any photos of Mr. Mercur— I mean, your son."

"I know," she said sadly, taking a sip of tea. "He won't let me keep any of them up anywhere. It's such a shame as he really is a handsome boy. From the right angle, anyway, and when he tucks in his shirt and shines his shoes. But he burned most of the photos I had."

"Has he always been a teacher?" I asked. "He was . . . so good at it."

"Yes, it was his calling," she said wistfully. "He's done a few jobs here and there, you know, while he was working out what he wanted to do with his life. I always knew he'd end up in something to do with science. That's where he really stood out."

"Did he make any friends when he was in prison?" Fred asked. "Anyone he might contact in times of need?"

Suzie kicked him in the shin and he yelped, looking at her in confusion.

"Prison?" Mrs. Silicon recoiled in horror. "My goodness, my boy has never gone to prison! He may be, well, a little useless, but he's certainly not a criminal. Whatever put that idea in your head?"

"Oh . . . um . . . now that I think about it, that school rumor was about a different teacher," Fred said, flustered.

"Yes, Fred, you're thinking of someone else," Suzie said through gritted teeth.

"My goodness, they had teachers at your school who had been in prison?" Mrs. Silicon tutted and took another sip of tea. "Things have changed since my day, that's for sure."

"It's nice that your son has always been into science," I said, steering the conversation back into focus. "Is he still teaching now?"

She let out a tired sigh. "No, he gave it up for some reason. I think he's very down about it. Whenever he's home, he spends all his time in his room. I don't know what he's up to in there; moping, I assume. I asked him to do the dusting last week, you know, to keep him busy, and did it get done? No. I've tried to encourage him to take up new hobbies, but he's gotten very lazy. And he's not musical like myself. I've just taken up the recorder. Another instrument to add to my impressive repertoire." She took a sip of tea and shook her head before continuing. "He just doesn't have quite the same drive as his sister."

"*Sister?*" I blurted out. "He has a sister?"

"Yes, an older sister," she said proudly. "She's very high achieving, but I'm afraid I can't say another word about what she does. It's *top secret*. Anyway, I do wish they'd get along, but you know what siblings can be like! Always in competition with each other. They've been that way since they were small."

"They don't get along?" I asked. "As in, Mr. Silicon wouldn't … I don't know… be with her right now, wherever she lives?"

She chuckled. "Oh no, absolutely not. They can't stand each other. And anyway, she travels a lot with her job. She hasn't seen him in years."

She took a sip of tea and then her face brightened as she gestured to the two framed certificates above the mantelpiece.

"I'm proud of both my children's achievements, even if they pretend the other one doesn't exist. You can see that Selena, my eldest, won an award for her dedication to, and excellence in, sports. She was always remarkably strong and agile. And next to it is the award Desmond got for his extraordinary talent in theater makeup and costume design."

"Mr. Silicon is trained in theater makeup," Georgie said, nodding as she stared at the certificate. "That makes sense."

"Growing up he was always very talented at transforming faces and dressing up. I thought he might go into the theater, you know, work in the West End, but then he decided on teaching." Her face brightened. "I have some more of his certificates upstairs if you'd like me to go get them for you to see?"

"Yes, please," Georgie enthused.

Mrs. Silicon looked delighted and bustled out of the room and up the stairs. I waited until she was gone and leaned forward, the others huddling round. Kimmy continued to stare intently at the plate of cookies, just in case one jumped off.

"I need to get into Mr. Mercury's room," I whispered. "She said he spends all his time up in his room when he's at home; there might be something important in there. I need to try to sneak in."

"We'll distract her when she comes back down so you can have a good look around without her getting suspicious," Georgie said firmly, the others nodding with her. "I have an idea as to how we can, too."

We heard Mrs. Silicon's footsteps coming back down the stairs and hurriedly returned to our relaxed poses on the sofas.

"Here we are!" Mrs. Silicon came bumbling in with some certificates and ribbons. "A long time ago, he was a high achiever. I don't know what happened."

"Mrs. Silicon, would you mind if we rearranged the room a little bit?" Georgie asked cheerily. "We'd like to put on a show for you and we need to push back the furniture."

Mrs. Silicon looked at her with a stunned expression. "A show?"

"Yes," Georgie nodded. "You've inspired me with those certificates of Mr. Silicon's achievements in theater costume. You see, I put on a fashion show earlier this term and I would have loved Mr. Silicon to have seen it. You'll need to imagine all the costumes, but would you like to see the performance?"

"I would LOVE to see it!" Mrs. Silicon said, clapping her hands. "Des would be so proud of you!"

The Bright Sparks jumped into action, pushing the furniture back to create space for a catwalk. Fred went to stand by the light switch and practiced switching it on and off again, before asking Mrs. Silicon to borrow a flashlight for the spotlight. Georgie took Suzie into the back corner of the room and got some accessories out of her bag, giving them to Suzie to put on, before styling Suzie's hair with her trusty can of hair spray. While being preened, Suzie did her breathing exercises, ready to launch into her cartwheels. Kizzy pushed back Mrs. Silicon's armchair and then led her to her seat, before pulling up another seat for Kimmy to hop up onto next to her, creating the audience.

"I'm just going to pop to the bathroom," I said breezily, heading out of the room.

I hurried up the stairs and heard music come on from the sitting room and a round of applause from Mrs. Silicon. I knew they wouldn't be able to keep the fashion show going for too long; I had to be quick. Ignoring Mrs. Silicon's bedroom, which I assumed was the bigger one with floral wallpaper and a vase of roses on the dressing table, I darted into the second-biggest bedroom with the unmade bed and a chemistry textbook resting on the bedside table.

My eyes immediately fell on the computer in the corner of the room, sitting on an empty desk. I switched it on and the last thing that he'd been looking at popped up on the screen: it was a website about Vatican City. It seemed an odd thing to be googling. Mrs. Silicon hadn't mentioned anything about going to Italy.

Hearing the music still playing downstairs and Mrs. Silicon's cheers and shouts for an encore, I got my phone out and called Nanny Beam.

"Hello, Aurora," she said, picking up. "I can't be too long as I'm in a crucially important meeting. Anything interesting about this new lead you told me about?"

"I'm not sure, maybe," I replied, clicking through the Vatican website. "Does Vatican City have anything to do with the precious stones?"

There was silence on the other end.

"Nanny Beam? Are you still there?"

"Yes," she said finally, her voice suddenly serious and urgent. "And yes, Vatican City does have something to do with the precious stones. How did you know?"

A feeling of dread washed over me as I scrolled down the web page that included maps of the Vatican and tourist information about its treasures.

"Because I think Mr. Mercury is planning a trip there. He may be there already. Why is the Vatican—"

"I believe the Heart of Love is set into the papal tiara. Aurora, the pope is its guardian."

My breath caught in my throat. "I need to get there right now. He's in danger."

"Stay where you are," Nanny Beam instructed. "Your transportation is already on its way."

"Seat belt, please."

I did as Aunt Lucinda instructed, clipping in my seat belt and making myself comfortable in the front seat of a bright-turquoise-blue car. I looked out the window to wave goodbye to the Bright Sparks standing outside Mrs. Silicon's house. Aunt Lucinda slammed her foot on the accelerator and we sped away from them at great speed. Alfred was in the back, strapped in and wearing a cloth napkin around his neck for some reason.

When Nanny Beam told me transportation was on the way, I'd expected a shiny black car full of MI5 agents to show up to take me to the airport. The Bright Sparks and I had been a little stunned when Aunt Lucinda had shown up, tooting the horn and telling me to get in.

"New car?" I asked. "What happened to the pink one?"

"Nanny Beam gave me an upgrade," she said, placing her sunglasses on and switching gear.

"Does it fly?"

Aunt Lucinda caught Alfred's eye in the rearview mirror.

"*Does it fly?*" she repeated, smirking. "Let's see, shall we?"

I braced myself as she pressed the large red button on the dashboard and wings sprang from the sides of the car. Automatic over-the-shoulder restraints came down over us,

strapping us to the seat like we were on a roller coaster.

A robotic voice spoke out of the car's surround sound system: "Flight mode engaged. Prepare for takeoff."

Aunt Lucinda, Alfred and I were slammed back against our seats as the car accelerated and took off, soaring into the air. Aunt Lucinda calmly took the wheel and a map came up on the screen, displaying the route to Vatican City.

"Whoa." I breathed out, the adrenaline pumping through my veins as I peered down at the houses below that were getting smaller as we flew higher. "That was awesome."

"Alfred is a big fan of the new car, aren't you, darling?" she called back to him.

I swiveled in my seat to see that he was fast asleep. He was also wearing an eye mask that he hadn't had on earlier. I was impressed that in the short time slot of our takeoff, he'd managed to find and put on an eye mask AND fall fast asleep. It had barely been a minute.

"He can sleep anywhere," Aunt Lucinda told me, looking at him affectionately in the rearview mirror. "It's quite a talent."

"Why is he wearing a napkin?"

"I told him we were off to Italy and he put it on straightaway. He is SUCH a fan of Italian food, but he's always getting pasta sauce down his front."

One of the screens on the dashboard started flashing green and a robotic voice announced, "Incoming Call: Kiyana Beam."

"Accept," Aunt Lucinda said.

Mum's worried face popped up on the screen. "Aurora! Are you all right? Nanny Beam just called."

"Yes, Aunt Lucinda and I are heading to Italy."

"I'm going to try to join you, so you don't have to do this alone. I'm in the middle of a mission and I . . . ah, wait one second—"

Mum ducked, and something strongly resembling a giant fireball went soaring past the screen.

"Mum! What was that? Are you OK?"

"Yes, nothing to worry about," she said, her hair slightly frazzled at the top. I watched as she held up her hands and shot several light energy blasts out.

"Kiyana, WHAT is going on?" Aunt Lucinda asked.

"Like I said, I'm in the middle of a mission." Mum rolled her eyes. "Someone has tried to fix the lack of light in Berkshire by inventing a machine that shoots fire up into the sky. He said he thought it would hold the darkness at bay. Unfortunately, the machine has taken on a mind of its own and gone ever-so-slightly out of control." She sighed. "I hate robots. Anyway, I'll be with you as soon as I can."

"Mum, listen, I can handle this. Aunt Lucinda and Alfred are with me and it looks like your hands are full."

A fireball went flying past her left ear. "But—"

"It's OK, Mum, really," I insisted as she dodged another fireball. "I've got this."

"And I'll be here to watch over her, Kiyana!" Aunt Lucinda trilled.

Mum looked terrified. "That's hardly a comfort, Lucinda."

Aunt Lucinda rolled her eyes and I smiled at the screen. "You stick with that mission and we'll keep you updated on ours."

"All right, if you're sure," Mum said. "Good luck and call me if you need to."

"Good luck with the fire robot!" Aunt Lucinda said cheerily, before hanging up.

I sat back in my seat. "How long will it take to get us to Italy?"

"Not long. On the way, you can tell me everything you know because Nanny Beam didn't exactly give me much detail. She just told me to pick you up and get to the Vatican." She steered slightly to the left, gliding over the clouds. "She told me you think Mr. Mercury might be hoping to add another crown to his collection?"

"That's right." I nodded. "I think he's going to steal the papal tiara."

"Which one?"

"What?" I stared at her. "There's more than one papal tiara?"

She looked at me as though I was mad. "Of course! The pope has been given many tiaras and such exquisite gifts throughout history."

"Argh!" I quickly googled it on my phone and started scrolling through the results, hoping for something to leap out at me. "This is when I need Kizzy! She'd probably know all the facts off by heart or have a book that had all the information."

"Excuse *you*," Aunt Lucinda said, sitting taller in her seat, "but you happen to be sitting in a car with two of the most brilliant jewel thieves in the country."

I raised my eyebrows at her, glancing up from my phone.

"Don't look at me like that, Aurora," she said defensively. "I borrow the jewels and always give them back. And I only keep the ones that are rightfully mine in the first place."

"Still, I don't think that's really something you should be bragging about."

"I'm not bragging, Aurora; I'm telling you that I may be able to help," she huffed. "Of course, Alfred is really the expert on these things, but I'd rather not wake him to ask. I have learned never to wake an ostrich in the middle of a nap on a flight. I did it once on our way to Dubai and he was so upset that I'd disturbed his dream about being the first ostrich to land on the moon that he stomped up and down the airplane, knocking everyone's drinks over onto their laps. Honestly, the dry-cleaning bill I was given was quite something."

"You know about the papal tiaras?" I asked hopefully, putting my phone down. "Do you have any idea which one Mr. Mercury would be after?"

"Oh yes. Now, all of them are quite desirable of course, but if I was Mr. Mercury I would want to steal the Napoleon Tiara," she said, her eyes sparkling with excitement. "It's beautiful, darling. Adorned with rubies, emeralds and sapphires, it was QUITE the crown."

"Was?"

She let out a long sigh. "Of course, Pope Benedict XV had to go and ruin things by removing the jewels from it and replacing them with replicas made of colored glass. He sold the jewels to raise money for the victims of the First World War."

"That's not ruining things, that's amazing," I corrected her. "But that can't be the one Mr. Mercury wants to steal. He'd be going for one with *real* precious stones, not colored glass replicas."

I couldn't say it out loud, but I also knew that if popes were the guardians of the Heart of Love, like the British monarchy have been the guardians of the Jewel of Truth and Nobility, there isn't a chance that Pope Benedict XV would have had it removed to sell it.

"Ah, but you're forgetting the emerald."

"What emerald?"

Aunt Lucinda got a dreamy expression on her face as she steered us through the air.

"The great emerald is the stone that used to be in the oldest surviving papal tiara and was then set into the Napoleon Tiara. It is spectacular."

"And it's still there? It's not replaced by colored glass?"

"It's still there," she assured me.

"That's probably what Mr. Mercury is after," I said, thinking it must be the Heart of Love if it was the only one not to be replaced. "Thanks,

Aunt Lucinda, I can't believe how much you know about the papal tiaras."

"There's no need to look so surprised," she chuckled. "Wait till you see this emerald. It's beautiful and incredibly precious."

You have no idea, I thought, staring out the window at the clouds.

As we flew over Italy, getting closer to Vatican City, Aunt Lucinda leaned forward so she was hunched over the steering wheel, peering straight ahead, her eyebrows knitted together in confusion.

"What is it?" I asked, following her gaze.

But she didn't need to answer. Ahead of us, the sky was growing steadily darker directly over where the map was telling us to land. It looked like it was spreading too, as the blue skies around us started becoming overcast.

"I don't understand," Aunt Lucinda said, looking at the map on the screen. "I checked, and the weather was supposed to be nice today in the Vatican."

"We need to get there as fast as possible." I gulped, as Aunt Lucinda switched on the headlights full beam. "I don't have a good feeling about this."

As soon as we came in to land in Vatican City, I could tell that something was wrong. From above, we could see a large crowd growing in the square at the front of a grand church, and what looked like either security staff or Italian police putting up barriers, so they couldn't come any closer. A small part of me hoped that perhaps it was just a coincidence and maybe there was a celebrity or something in the church that the crowd was waiting for. A much larger part of me noted the skies above Vatican City growing darker and darker by the second.

My phone beeped with a message from

Nanny Beam.

> Can't get through to the pope. Will keep
> trying. My best agents are on the way,
> but you may get there before them.
> Keep me advised.

"Where do we go now?" Aunt Lucinda said, after we'd landed safely and our seat restraints automatically lifted.

We had attracted a lot of attention and tourists had stopped to stare as the car hovered just above the ground before neatly landing. Ignoring the camera phones pointing in my direction, I climbed out of the car and turned to Aunt Lucinda as she locked it.

"Where is that Napoleon Tiara kept?" I asked.

"Saint Peter's Basilica," she answered, pointing to the beautiful, grand church across the square where everyone was gathering. "It's on display there, I think."

"Come on," I said, running as fast as possible across the square, with Aunt Lucinda and Alfred hot on my heels.

I forced my way to the front of the crowd and leaned over the barrier to see what was going on. They had cordoned off the church and no one was being allowed in or out.

"This isn't a good sign," Aunt Lucinda said, before waving at one of the policemen to get their attention.

"Do you speak English?" she asked breathlessly as he approached.

He raised his eyebrows at Alfred, who had also barged his way to the front, much to the annoyance of everyone else. He was still wearing his napkin and he began pecking at a tourist's backpack in interest, before pulling out a sandwich and swallowing it whole, looking

very pleased with himself. The backpack's owner did NOT look pleased.

"Yes, I speak English," the policeman said with a strong Italian accent. "Is this your ostrich? He just stole that man's sandwich. And he is currently trying to steal that woman's watch."

"Never mind that, it's not important," Aunt Lucinda said, waving his accusations off. "Look, what's happened? Why aren't we allowed into the church? And also . . . are you single?"

"*Aunt Lucinda!*" I hissed as she fluttered her eyelashes at him. "Can we focus, please?"

"There's been a theft. No one is allowed in." He blushed. "And yes, I am single. Ciao."

"Ciao," Aunt Lucinda replied with a smile.

Seriously? AS IF THIS WAS A TIME FOR ROMANCE!

"What's been stolen?" I asked loudly, forcing him to break his dreamy gaze at my aunt and look down at me.

His eyes widened. "Aren't you *Ragazza Fulmine*? Lightning Girl?"

There was a ripple of whispers from those around us and people started craning their necks to get a look at me.

"Yes, I am. And it's really important that you tell me exactly what was taken."

He nodded. "Of course, Lightning Girl. I

am happy to tell you. The Napoleon Tiara was stolen about half an hour ago. We have no idea who the culprit is. All the lights went down in the church and everything just. . ."

"Blacked out? The work of the Blackout Burglar." I closed my eyes and shook my head, before looking up into the worried eyes of Aunt Lucinda. "We're too late. Mr. Mercury has already been here. We need to go and see—"

My phone's ringtone interrupted and I answered straightaway when I saw it was Nanny Beam.

"Aurora," she spoke down the phone hurriedly, "my agents have just gotten to the pope's private residence at the Apostolic Palace and it's been ransacked—"

"He found it," I said, cutting her off. "He may have looked for it there first, but we just got to St. Paul's Basilica and he's taken the Napoleon Tiara with the precious stone in it."

"He wasn't searching the pope's residence for the Heart of Love."

"What do you mean? What else did he want? That's the only thing that's been taken."

"No, it's not. He's taken the guardian too," she said, sounding panicked. "Aurora, the pope is missing."

10

"Aurora, what on earth is going on?"

Aunt Lucinda came running up behind me as I marched back to the car. Nanny Beam had told me she'd call back in a minute after she'd made her report to the Queen on the situation. Nanny Beam was adamant that we couldn't tell anyone about the pope yet. She had to keep it under wraps for as long as possible, knowing the panic that would erupt from the public the moment they found out.

"We have to go."

"Go where?"

"I'm not sure. Nanny Beam is going to call back, and we need to leave as soon as she tells us where to go, so we should wait in the car."

"What is this all about?" Aunt Lucinda threw her hands up in exasperation. "Something else is going on that you're not telling me. I know it's important to find Mr. Mercury and stop him from stealing more jewelry, but there's a lot more fuss around this whole operation than normal. And I would know. So tell me what's so important about that tiara he's taken."

"Where's Alfred?" I asked, standing at the car and looking round the square.

"Don't try to change the subject, Aurora, I won't be—" She hesitated, glancing around her. "Although, where has that ostrich gotten to? I hope he hasn't flounced off in one of his moods. Last time that happened, it took me two days to track him down and I eventually found him meditating in a Norwegian forest."

I opened the car door and got into the front seat, gripping my phone in my hands, terrified of missing Nanny Beam's call. Aunt Lucinda slid into the driver's seat and, giving up on getting more information from me, began to reapply her lipstick as we waited. I went online and saw that there were pictures of me getting out of the just-landed flying car and then more of me talking to the policeman outside the church. I sighed, leaning my head back on the headrest. I hadn't exactly done a good job of keeping a low profile; now everyone would be asking what I was doing there and why the crime of the stolen papal tiara was so important to Lightning Girl that I raced to the Vatican in a flying car.

Nanny Beam was going to have a job on her hands keeping the pope's situation out of the press. I felt sick with worry. Where would Mr.

Mercury have taken him? And how did he do it without anyone noticing?

"He had help," I said, answering my own question out loud.

"Who had help?" Aunt Lucinda asked, putting her makeup away.

"Mr. Mercury. He didn't do this alone. He's being helped by someone."

"He can't be. Darek Vermore is in prison."

I stared straight ahead of me. "Maybe Darek is helping him still from inside jail."

"That's unlikely," Aunt Lucinda commented. "Have you been to that prison? How could they possibly communicate? Darek is under constant watch."

We both jumped at the sound of the rear car door being opened and then slammed shut as Alfred returned.

"There you are, darling! Where have you been?"

Alfred opened his feathered wings and revealed a canvas that he propped up onto the seat next to him proudly.

Aunt Lucinda gasped. "Is that ... is that the *Madonna of Foligno*?"

"The what?" I asked, staring at the beautiful painting as Alfred wiggled his bottom feathers excitedly.

"The *Madonna of Foligno*," Aunt Lucinda whispered, her eyes twinkling. "A very, very

famous painting by Raphael. It's centuries old and completely . . . priceless."

"Alfred, tell me that's a copy that you just bought in the gift shop and you did not just STEAL a PRICELESS painting from the *Vatican*," I said slowly.

He stretched his neck forward to glare at me out of the side of his head with his big beady eye. Oh no. I buried my head in my hands.

"Oh darling, you are clever!" Aunt Lucinda told him in a soothing voice, unable to take her eyes off the painting. "But we'll have to return it, otherwise I'll never hear the end of it from Kiyana once Aurora tells her."

Suddenly the car started ringing and Nanny Beam's face popped up onto the screen at the front.

"Nanny Beam!" I exclaimed, swiveling forward. "Where do we need to go? You must tell me where the other one is."

"The other what?" Aunt Lucinda asked, reluctantly tearing her eyes from the canvas. "Really, what is going on?"

"You need to get to—" Nanny Beam hesitated, peering into the camera. "Is that the *Madonna of Foligno* on the back seat of the car next to Alfred?"

"Just a copy from the gift shop, Mummy!" Aunt Lucinda said shrilly, winking at me.

"Lucinda, this is a video call. I can see you winking at Aurora. And you make sure Alfred returns that at once. The French president is still smarting over the *Mona Lisa* incident." She turned her attention to me. "You need to get to India as fast as you can. To the Tsuglagkhang Temple in McLeod Ganj. I'm afraid I don't know where in the temple, but it's in there somewhere."

"We're on our way," I replied determinedly, clicking in my seat belt.

"Wait a second, we're going to India now?" Aunt Lucinda looked baffled. "But I haven't packed for India! I packed for Italy. I need a complete wardrobe overhaul if we're going to India!"

"Get there as fast as you can. In the meantime, I'll send some backup to help you. I'll tell them to meet you at the temple," Nanny Beam continued, ignoring Aunt Lucinda. "And I'll be sure to put some extra security on him."

"On who?" Aunt Lucinda and I chorused.

Nanny Beam took a deep breath and stared at me from the screen.

"The Dalai Lama."

*

Aunt Lucinda tried to encourage me to sleep in the car on the flight to India, but my brain was too busy. Every time I closed my eyes, I saw Mr. Mercury cackling, his eyes glinting with pleasure at having the precious stones in his grasp. And Alfred was snoring so loudly from the back seat, I probably wouldn't have been able to get any sleep anyway.

"We're here!" Aunt Lucinda announced as the wheels touched the ground after a few hours, causing Alfred to sit bolt upright and bang his head on the roof of the car.

"Oh dear," Aunt Lucinda sighed, looking at him sympathetically in the rearview mirror, "he'll be in a terrible mood all day now."

"You mean, all night?" I said, undoing my seat belt, desperate to get out of the car and stretch my legs. "It's dark out."

Aunt Lucinda pointed to the local time that was flashing up on the dashboard screen.

"Well, it shouldn't be. It's the middle of the day."

I opened the car door and got out, looking up at the gray, shadowed sky. This wasn't a good sign.

"Aurora?"

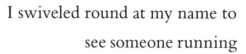

I swiveled round at my name to see someone running toward me from outside the temple. Someone with dark hair dyed bright neon blue at the ends and headphones around her neck as always.

"CHERRY!"

She pulled me in for a hug and then stepped back to grin at me.

"It's so good to see you!"

"What are you doing here?" I asked, already feeling better about everything just at the sight of her.

"Nanny Beam called and arranged for me to fly here from Malaysia. She said something big was going on and that you could probably use some support. Not that I was surprised to receive her call."

"You heard about what happened in Rome?"

She shook her head. "No, but I had a premonition a few hours before Nanny Beam got in touch. I've never had one like that before. It was so bad, it made my vision blurry and I went into a bit of a daze. I thought I could even make out shapes of people at one point."

"Cherry, how lovely to see you," Aunt Lucinda said, swanning over. "Do you have any idea what's going on or is it only me who is in the dark?"

"I don't have a clue, I'm just here for support," Cherry explained. "Speaking of being in the dark, do you know what's going on with the sky?"

"We need to go into the temple. Come on," I said, leading the way toward the beautiful Tsuglagkhang Temple. "There's something there that Mr. Mercury is after."

"Wow," Cherry whispered when we got to the

doorway, her eyes widening as she took in all the bright colors, the murals and paintings, and the prayer flags of the temple. It truly was breathtaking.

At the far end was a large golden Buddha statue behind a throne, where the Dalai Lama sat when giving his teachings. Glancing round

the temple from the doorway, my eyes kept being drawn back to the throne as though it was exuding a powerful energy.

"So, when we go in, what exactly are we looking for?" Cherry asked, turning to me.

"Anything that you think Mr. Mercury might want to steal," I whispered back, taking off my shoes. "Or if it looks like something is missing."

While Aunt Lucinda and Cherry went off in one direction, I walked straight down the middle of the serenely silent temple toward the throne. I stopped in front of it and admired the amazingly detailed depictions carved all around the edge until my eyes stopped at the bottom right-hand corner. Something didn't quite match the rest. There was a jagged indent, about the size of a large pebble, and as I peered closer at it, I saw scratch marks around the hole, as though a knife had been used to gouge something out of the throne.

My stomach dropped and I quickly turned on my heel, gesturing for Aunt Lucinda and Cherry to follow me outside. I knew exactly what had been cut out of that throne: the Gem of Wisdom and Peace.

"What is it?" Cherry asked, her brow furrowed in concern. "Did you see something?"

"We need to find the Dalai Lama straightaway," I replied, causing Cherry and Aunt Lucinda to share a worried look. "He's in danger. Cherry, if you could put on your headphones and maybe use your supersonic hearing to find out where he is in the complex, we can find him and—"

My sentence was cut off by a roaring sound coming from overhead and what felt like a strong wind blustering around us. We all looked up into the sky to see a helicopter taking off. A feeling of dread ran through me as it hovered

above us threateningly and then flew away, far into the distance.

Just moments later, my phone rang and Nanny Beam's name popped up on the screen.

"Aurora, you need to leave immediately," she instructed, before I'd even managed to say hello. "The Dalai Lama has been kidnapped. My agents have just confirmed it."

I closed my eyes in horror, unable to say

anything. He was on that helicopter. We had just missed him, minutes behind Mr. Mercury. If only I had gotten here sooner.

"Aurora, are you there?" Nanny Beam said in a panicked voice.

"Yes, I'm here."

"You need to leave. Tell Aunt Lucinda and Cherry to get in that car and bring you straight home to Hertfordshire. We have to protect you. The Dalai Lama and the pope have both been kidnapped; that means the last two guardians are you and the Queen. He'll be after you next. I have to go, but let me know when you're on your way."

She hung up.

"I've just gotten a hundred messages from Mummy saying I'm to take you home," Aunt Lucinda told me, nodding toward the car where Alfred was still standing, determined to dent the offending roof. "Alfred, stop pecking at the roof, will you, darling? It's completely bulletproof and explosion proof, so I imagine it can withstand ostrich beaks. You're just tiring yourself for no reason."

"Come on, Aurora," Cherry said, glancing nervously up at the darkening sky. "Let's get you home. I've got a bad feeling about all this."

"We can go home, but we need to make a stop on the way," I replied.

"Oh?" Aunt Lucinda raised her eyebrows. "Why?"

"Because that's not the first time I've seen a helicopter exactly like that one fly into the distance," I explained, marching determinedly toward the car. "And this time round, I know exactly who owns it."

11

"I hoped I would see you again soon, Aurora."

Darek watched me carefully as I sat down opposite him.

"Have you had time to think about—"

"Tell me about the Dalai Lama," I interrupted, leaning forward and fixing him with my most determined stare. "Where has Mr. Mercury taken him and the pope?"

Handcuffed to the table, he linked his fingers together and looked down at his lap, avoiding eye contact.

"Darek!" I snapped. "You need to tell me where they are, NOW. I know it's you that is behind all this."

He looked up.

"What makes you think that?"

"Because I watched the helicopter fly off with the Dalai Lama and I recognized it from the Superhero Conference last year," I explained, narrowing my eyes at him. "It was the same helicopter that took off with the Light of the World."

"I can't help you, Aurora." He sighed. "Not until you help me."

"How are you instructing Mr. Mercury from inside the prison? Who else is helping him? Is it an employee from Vermore Enterprises? You know that we'll find them, Darek, so you might as well tell me now who it is."

"If you get me out of prison, I'll tell you everything."

"You know I can't do that!" I practically yelled, growing more and more agitated. "I would never help you after everything you did."

"But I'm sorry about all that!" he wailed, clenching his hands. "I made a mistake!"

His tone completely took me aback. I stared at him in shocked silence as his eyes filled with tears. He looked so vulnerable.

"I told you," he croaked, "I regret it all. Can't you see I've learned my lesson? I don't want to be here anymore and the only way I'm ever getting out of prison is by bargaining with you using the information I have. If you get me out of prison, I'll help you."

"I'm not going to fall for this," I said sternly, telling myself more than him because for a moment I really did start to believe that maybe he was truly sorry. "I'm not. Now, last time I was here, I saw that you had been visited by someone who had just written 'N' in the visitors' logbook. Is that Mr. Mercury in disguise? Is that how you've been telling him what to do from inside here?"

A shadow fell across Darek's face as I mentioned the mysterious visitor. He pursed his lips tightly and shook his head, not saying a word.

"What disguise is Mr. Mercury using to—"

"I am NOT working with Mr. Mercury!" Darek growled, slamming his hand on the table. "That man is despicable, and that he should be anywhere near those precious stones makes my blood boil. He doesn't deserve any of it."

"He's not working for you? Do you know who he is working with? Or where I can find him? I know he can't have done all this on his own. It must be you who is behind it. Who else could possibly help him with the resources and knowledge about the precious stones? It was

YOUR helicopter that I saw!"

Darek's eyes glanced up to meet mine for just a moment before returning to focus on his clenched fists.

"I'm not saying anything else," he said. "Not until you get me out of this place."

"This is serious," I said in a softer tone, desperately attempting a different tactic. "He has kidnapped the Dalai Lama and the pope. I need answers."

"And I need you to trust that I am a changed man," he replied, his voice breaking with emotion. "I can help you return the Light of the World to where it needs to go."

I blinked at him. "What?"

"The Light of the World," he repeated. "Have you returned it yet? To maintain the proper balance of light and dark in the world, that precious-stones book says you must take it back to where Dawn Beam discovered it.

The safety of every person on the planet is at stake. It said so in that precious-stones book. I remember reading about it in there."

"And I will do that when I can. But, in case you haven't noticed, a madman has been going around the world stealing precious stones and their guardians, so I haven't thought about it lately."

"Really?" He raised his eyebrows at me. "I would have thought that's exactly why you should be thinking about it. If Mr. Mercury has gotten his grubby hands on the other precious stones, what makes you think he isn't coming after the Light of the World?"

"It's safe."

"Like the others were?"

I didn't say anything. Darek knew he had hit a nerve and leaned forward across the table, keeping his voice low even though there was no one but us in the room.

"I know where the Light of the World needs to be returned to: under the aurora borealis. That's the only place it will be safe and restore the balance of light and dark."

"How could you possibly know where Dawn Beam originally found it?" I asked.

"Because I know everything about that stone. Even more than its guardian." He paused, giving me a gentle smile. "I've dedicated my life to it, as you know. Without me, you wouldn't have even known you were the guardian in the first place."

His eyes flickered to where my hands were resting on the table. I turned over my left hand to face my palm upward so that the swirled scar was visible.

"It really is amazing," he said softly, staring at the scar. "You have no idea just how powerful you are, Aurora."

"Mr. Mercury wouldn't dare come after the Light of the World," I said, shoving my hands under the table and bringing the conversation back into focus. "He knows how well guarded it is."

Darek shook his head. "The only place it is really safe is underneath the aurora borealis, where it belongs. Your role as guardian is to protect it. If you don't take it back there, that precious stone will go missing along with all the others. Mr. Mercury will have won and then. . ." He looked pained, his whole face scrunching up as his sentence fizzled out.

"Aurora," he said, snapping his head back up, "break me out of prison and I can take you."

"Break you out of prison? Have you lost your mind?"

"That's the only way!"

"You must think I'm crazy," I said, pushing my chair back and standing up. "I came here for answers, thinking that there might be just one tiny bit of goodness left in you, but I was wrong. You're going to be stuck in here forever."

"I meant it when I said I had learned my lesson!" he cried, his pleading tone stopping me from walking right out of there. "You think I want Mr. Mercury to have that kind of power?"

He let out a loud "HA!" and buried his head in his hands. I stood in silence for a moment, not quite sure what to do, but then he lifted his head and spoke again.

"I don't want the power for *me*," he said, his eyes locking with mine. "I want to help my family. I made a terrible mistake and I am sorry for it. I am telling you the truth."

"If you mean that, you'd tell me where the Dalai Lama and the pope are. You'd help me to recover the precious stones Mr. Mercury already has."

"Please, just think about it," he said solemnly. "Get me out of here and I'll take you to return the Light of the World to where it belongs. That's the only place it will be safe and that's the only way of bringing all of this to an end."

I walked over to the door and left the room before he could say anything else. The prison officer waiting just outside gave me a strange look.

"Everything all right, Lightning Girl?"

I nodded. "Yes. Thank you."

But I was lying. Everything was not all right. As Aunt Lucinda drove Cherry and me away from the prison toward home, I couldn't shake a horribly unsettling feeling.

The feeling that Darek Vermore may just have been making sense.

12

I was so bored.

Mum kept telling me that lying low was for my own safety, but it felt a little bit like I was under house arrest, especially since Nanny Beam had posted a load of agents around our house to keep watch. On the third day of not being allowed to go to school, I mentioned my take on the situation to Dad as he started cooking dinner.

"Don't be ridiculous, Aurora, you are not under house arrest," Dad said and chuckled. "We're just taking a few precautions, that's all.

Nanny Beam pointed out that Mr. Mercury knows your school very well, having been in disguise there for a while. We don't want to take any risks."

Kimmy barked loudly in agreement from her bed nearby. She'd spent the last three days following me from room to room, thrilled that I was now at home during the day so she could keep an eye on me all the time. I'd told Nanny Beam that she didn't need to make her agents stand out in the cold all day protecting the house when we had Kimmy to do that, but she hadn't listened.

"And," Dad continued, his eyes twinkling, "at least you have plenty of company. Cherry, Aunt Lucinda, Alfred..."

He trailed off as we heard a loud crash from upstairs. Aunt Lucinda had mentioned to us a few minutes ago that Alfred was going to use Mum and Dad's bedroom for his online Zumba class.

"Oh dear," Dad sighed, raising his eyes to the ceiling and grimacing at the loud bass coming through from Alfred's speakers. "That sounds like a few broken photo frames. Anyway, what was I saying? Ah, yes, that you've got some great company to join you in putting... uh" – he paused and then waggled his finger at my face – "whatever that is on your face."

"It's a homemade oatmeal and coconut milk face mask," I explained, leaning back against the counter and picking up a spoon to look at my reflection. "Aunt Lucinda made it for us."

"Hey, Aurora, I think you have some messages," Cherry said, wandering in from the sitting room, her face also slathered in an oatmeal face mask. "Your phone vibrated a couple of times."

She passed me my phone, which I'd left with her on the sofa, and I saw that the messages were from the Bright Sparks, asking how I was feeling. Like everyone else at school, they thought I'd been struck down with a terrible flu and so was stuck in bed for the week. I'd told them that it was super contagious so not to come to the house. My heart sank as I read their get-better-soon messages and I felt an overwhelming sense of guilt.

I WISHED I could tell them everything. Lying to the Bright Sparks was so weird and I hated doing it, but I also knew that it was too complicated to let them in on all this. I couldn't even tell Aunt Lucinda and Cherry exactly what had happened in the Vatican and India, and they had been there in person. Nanny Beam had explained to them that Mr. Mercury was up to something and kidnapping prominent public figures appeared to be part of his plan. At least I could talk to Mum about it, but it was difficult to speak without the risk of being overheard, considering how many people were crowded into the house.

"Wouldn't it be easier to just tell them the truth?" I had asked Nanny Beam when she'd popped over to the house to speak to Aunt Lucinda and Cherry, before instructing Mum and Dad not to let me out of their sight.

She had put a hand on my shoulder and given me a sad smile.

"This isn't about doing what's easy," she'd said. "It's about protecting the precious stones and their powers."

I knew that she was right, but lying to the Bright Sparks wasn't something that came to me naturally.

"Suzie won another gymnastics competition," I announced to Dad and Cherry, reading through their school updates. "And apparently Fred has detention. Again."

"What did he do this time?" Dad asked, putting on the oven timer.

"He meant to throw a water balloon at Suzie,

missed, and hit a school inspector square in the face," I read out loud, causing Cherry and Dad to burst out laughing. "I wish I could have seen that."

Kimmy suddenly got up from her bed and ran to the front door, wagging her tail and barking in excitement, something she only does when it's a family member coming home. Dad checked his watch.

"Right on time. Mum's home."

I glanced at the time on my phone and looked back at Dad in confusion.

"I thought she was going straight from her meeting with MI5 to pick up Alexis and Clara from school. But school hasn't finished yet."

Dad grinned. "Why don't you two go get the door for her?"

Cherry shrugged, looking as baffled as I did. We made our way down the hall and could hear Mum's voice as she spoke to the agents stationed outside the door and then another muffled voice speaking to them, too.

"Who is that?" Cherry asked.

I pulled Kimmy, who was by now bounding up and down in excitement, out of the way, and opened the front door to see Mum on the doorstep searching for the keys in her bag.

"Hey, Aurora," she said, beaming. "I just swung by the airport and guess who I happened to find there?"

She stepped aside to reveal the person standing right behind her.

"JJ!" I cried, lunging at him to give him a hug. "What are you doing here?"

"You thought I was going to let you and

Cherry have an adventure on your own?" He laughed as he was ushered into the hallway by Mum, offering Cherry a high five. "When Cherry told me that Nanny Beam had asked her to get to India because of a sighting of Mr. Mercury there or whatever, I told my parents that Lightning Girl needed my help and they agreed to let me fly here as long as your parents were happy with it."

Mum smiled and put her arm round my shoulders. "I thought you could do with some cheering up. JJ and I decided it would be a good surprise."

"Thanks, Mum. You're the best," I said, as she kissed the top of my head.

Cherry nodded. "Nicely done, Mrs. Beam."

"You can call me Kiyana," Mum corrected.

"The agents around your house are kind of scary," JJ noted. "They searched me and everything. I asked if I could try on the guy's sunglasses, but he was very serious."

"You can't just ask an MI5 agent to try on his sunglasses," Cherry said, rolling her eyes.

"Whatever, they would have looked good on me. I also tried challenging him to arm wrestling, but Mrs. Beam wouldn't let me."

"Kiyana," Mum corrected again. "And I felt that it might be a little unfair, what with you having super strength. The last thing we need is for the agents sent here to protect us losing confidence in their abilities after losing at arm wrestling."

"Anyway, the most important question I have for you right now is" – JJ inhaled deeply for a dramatic pause – "can someone tell me why you both have weird-looking slime all over your faces?"

"It's actually a very relaxing and soothing homemade face mask," Aunt Lucinda said, breezing into the hall from the sitting room, carrying a bowl of the mixture. "Would you like some?"

"Are you kidding?" A wide grin spread across his face. "I've just been on a flight from Nigeria to London and then searched by MI5 agents. Pass me the slime."

*

That night, I was woken up by Cherry mumbling in her sleep. Mum had set up a mattress in my room for her to sleep on and JJ was on the sofa downstairs, while Aunt Lucinda and Alfred were both in the spare room. It may have been a little squished in the house, but even my parents had to admit it was a lot of fun with everyone staying there.

"Cherry? Are you awake?" I whispered.

She didn't reply, but instead continued to talk nonsense in her sleep. I smiled to myself and rolled over, nestling back into my pillow. But her voice got louder and then there was a moment's silence before she said a name so clearly that a shiver ran down my spine.

"*Mercury.*"

Jolting in her sleep, Cherry began crying out. I pulled my duvet off and knelt to shake her awake, but she swatted me off.

My bedroom door swung open and JJ, Mum and Dad came rushing into the room.

"What's going on?" Mum asked, switching on the light. "Is everything all right?"

"I think Cherry is having a really bad nightmare. I can't wake her up!"

Cherry woke with a start and sat bolt upright. She blinked at me and then everyone standing in the doorway, her eyebrows knitted in confusion.

"Are you OK? You were having a nightmare," I explained, as she slowed her breathing and then wiped her forehead.

"Yes, sorry, just a bad dream," she said, realizing what was going on and looking up at my parents apologetically. "I'm so sorry that I woke you."

"Not at all," Dad said, yawning.

"Are you OK, Cherry? Would you like a glass of water?" Mum asked.

Cherry shook her head. "No, I'm fine. Thank you."

"We'll get back to bed then," Mum said, as Dad plodded back to their bedroom. "Night, everyone."

"Night," we chorused, before she shut the door behind her.

"See you in the morning then," JJ said, heading to the door.

"Wait," Cherry said as he reached for the handle. "I need to tell you two something. I didn't have a nightmare."

JJ and I shared a look of confusion and then he sat down at the end of her mattress, ready to listen. Cherry bit her lip. She looked shaken by whatever it was that had happened.

"What's going on?" I asked. "Was it a premonition?"

"It wasn't a premonition. It was a vision. A real *vision*. I've never had one before."

"A vision, as in ... you saw the future?" JJ said, watching her in awe.

"I don't know." She looked at me worriedly. "Normally, I just feel if something bad is going to happen. That's how my premonitions have

always worked. But this was so different...
It's like my powers are warning me about how
dangerous things really are, or how dangerous
they could be, by showing me exactly what's
happening. It sounds silly, I know."

"It doesn't sound silly at all," I said firmly,
JJ nodding in agreement. "I think that makes
perfect sense. What was your vision? I heard
you say the word 'Mercury' during it."

She took a deep breath, her eyes fixed on
her hands resting in her lap as she focused on
remembering it.

"Mr. Mercury was in a tunnel, maybe
underground or he dug through a cave or
something. It was very dark, and he was holding
a flashlight. He walked into a room, which was
so dimly lit, I couldn't really see anything.
There was ... a person in the corner with a hood
over their face."

She pursed her lips, closing her eyes. Neither

JJ or I said anything, both of us completely enraptured and waiting for the rest of the story.

"I could feel how scared Mr. Mercury was," she continued, clutching her stomach. "I could *feel* it. He was terrified. The hooded figure told Mr. Mercury to turn off his flashlight and as Mr. Mercury fumbled for the switch, he dropped it. It shone a light right at them."

"Did you see who it was?" I asked gently as she paused.

She shook her head. "I just saw their hand."

"Their hand?"

"When the light shone at them, they jumped away, crying out in anger until Mr. Mercury snatched the flashlight up from the ground and turned it off. Then the person held their hand out from the shadows; I could just see it in the glow from one of the lanterns. Mr. Mercury put a stone into their hand. The hand was scarred."

"What did the stone look like?" I asked.

"I couldn't really see it. But then they told Mr. Mercury that there was just one more to get. They said that he had to move quickly before it was safely returned and out of his reach forever. Mr. Mercury asked the hooded figure's advice on how he was going to get it and then . . . I woke up."

We sat in silence, digesting the information Cherry had just given us.

"What do you think it means, Aurora?" JJ asked finally.

They both looked at me expectantly and I shook my head.

"I'm not sure," I told them honestly. "But I think I know what we need to do next."

The first thing I did the next morning was to call a family meeting.

"This had better be important," Alexis yawned, plonking himself down on the sofa next to Clara after I'd dragged him from his room. "I was just about to get to level 108 in this new game I've been asked to test."

"Tell me you weren't up all night playing computer games?" Mum asked, sitting on the arm of the sofa and giving him one of her best stern-mum looks.

"Don't worry, Aunt Lucinda has already promised to make a revitalizing smoothie for me, so I won't feel tired today," he replied smugly.

"Where's Dad?" I asked impatiently, absent-mindedly stroking Kimmy's ears as she took her place at my feet. "I need everyone to be here before we can get started."

"I saw him chasing Alfred round the garden," Clara told me without looking up from the science book open on her lap. "I think Alfred stole his entire collection of ties."

Mum laughed and then stood up to go through to the garden. "I'll go get them. Back in a sec."

Alexis waited until Mum was out of the room to raise his eyebrows at me.

"So, little sis, what's this all about then?"

"You'll find out soon enough," I assured him. "I'm actually hoping that you'll be able to give up your free time to help me out today, Alexis. I need your computer genius. It's important."

"Where are Cherry and JJ?" Clara asked, still not looking up from her book. "Aren't they invited to the family meeting?"

"They're already aware of the particulars. Aunt Lucinda is giving them a yoga lesson upstairs," I said, taking a few gulps of my coconut water in the hope that it would help to wake me up. I was feeling a strange mixture of tiredness from staying up so late talking things through with Cherry and JJ, and tingling nerves from the adrenaline pumping through me as I thought about what I was going to try to do.

"Does this meeting have something to do with Cherry yelling in her sleep last night?" Alexis asked curiously. "I was just hitting level fifty-four when I heard it."

There was a commotion as Alfred came

stomping down the corridor past the sitting room, wiggling his bottom feathers indignantly and wearing a load of ties round his long neck. As he went upstairs, Mum came in from the kitchen with Dad in tow, who was red in the face and had to lean on the door frame for a moment, bent double, trying to catch his breath.

"Everything OK, Dad?" Alexis asked, trying and failing to suppress a smirk.

"That … ostrich … is … going … to … kill … me," he wheezed.

I passed him my glass of coconut water and he gratefully took the last few swigs before moving Alexis along and slumping down onto the sofa next to him.

"Don't worry, darling," Mum said soothingly, putting a hand on his shoulder. "You've been needing a closet clear-out for a while. We'll get you some new ties."

Dad looked up at her with a pleading expression. "When did you say your sister was moving out again?"

I cleared my throat and Kimmy barked, ensuring that everyone was paying attention.

"I called this family meeting as I have something very important to discuss." I took a deep breath and looked at Mum and Dad. "At the beginning of the year, you told me that you trusted me and that you were going to let me go ahead and do what I could to find Mr. Mercury, but the deal was I had to keep you in the loop. You wanted to all work together this time round. Right?"

"Right," Mum said, Dad nodding in agreement.

"I considered not telling you what I'm about to say," I admitted, hesitating before Kimmy rested her head in my lap in encouragement. "But I think you're right; it's better to work together and I definitely could do with your help."

"What's going on, Aurora?" Dad asked gently, the pink in his cheeks slowly fading as his heart rate returned to normal.

"You told me that you trusted me, and I need you to trust me right now." I paused, trying to think of the best way of saying it before deciding to just blurt it out plain and simple. "I need you to give me the Light of the World."

Dad and Mum stared at me. Clara finally glanced up from her book and Alexis smiled, looking impressed.

"You want us to give you the Light of the World," Dad repeated slowly. "Why?"

"Because it's time that I started acting like its guardian," I answered determinedly. "The world is getting darker every day; strange things are happening, and I think it has something to do with the Beams' precious stone. I want to fix things and I have an idea of how. I know you might not believe me, but I can handle this. I *know* I can."

There was a moment's silence as Mum and Dad shared a knowing look, as though they were both thinking exactly the same thing. I prepared myself for a gentle put-down lecture, but that wasn't what happened.

"Aurora," Mum said, a smile creeping across her face, "you may not believe *us*, but we know you can handle it."

"Dad, are you . . . crying?" Alexis asked.

Dad sniffed, dabbing his eyes with his sleeve. "It's just, we're so proud of you, Aurora. You're so brave and determined, and only twelve years old! You really are a superhero, with or without your powers."

"Your dad's right," Mum said, taking his hand and squeezing it. "And I'm really proud that you haven't gone behind our backs this time and you've asked us straight out. If *you* think it's time for you to take the Light of the World, then *I* trust that it's time."

Alexis blinked at me. "Seriously, this is NOT the reaction I got when I asked to skip school to go to a technology convention. I didn't go behind your backs then, and yet I didn't get a watery-eyed smile and a speech about how proud everyone was of me."

"Yes, well, that was *slightly* different." Mum

laughed, reaching over to ruffle his hair. "And this doesn't come without conditions."

"And those conditions are?" I asked in my most sophisticated, grown-up voice.

"Whatever your plan is, you don't go it alone," Dad said. "You have a tendency to try to take on dangerous situations by yourself, and the Bright Sparks have to insist on joining you. If you're taking the Light of the World anywhere, someone is going with you. There are MI5 agents surrounding our house for a reason – I want you to be safe."

Mum nodded. "Absolutely. We'll give you the Light of the World, but we want to help protect it."

"Deal," I said, with a wave of relief at this being their condition. "I was planning on asking you to come along with me, Mum, anyway. You're the proper Beam superhero after all; I'm going to need all the help I can get on the way."

"So, you'll let us in on the full plan of what you're going to do with the stone once you have it?" Dad checked.

"Yes. Definitely."

Mum beamed at me and Dad stood up, clapping his hands together.

"Right then," he announced. "Let's go get the Light of the World. Follow me."

We all stood up and followed Mum and Dad into the kitchen, and then through to the small boot room by the back door that led out to the garden.

"This is so exciting," Clara whispered to me, taking my hand. "Thanks for including me in this family meeting, even though you didn't need to."

"Oh yes I did," I said, squeezing her hand. "Your role in all this is still to come."

"Are you ready?" Mum asked, turning to me,

Clara and Alexis as we formed a little semicircle behind them, squeezing into the small room.

"Mum," I said slowly, glancing around us, "please tell me you haven't been keeping the most precious stone in the world . . . in our *boot room*?"

"Actually, we have," Dad said. "Not just anywhere, mind you."

He reached for Kimmy's dry dog food bag sitting on the shelf in the corner and plonked it in front of us. Kimmy barked happily, jumping up and down at the sight of it and then running around in circles, chasing her tail in excitement.

"Ta-da!"

Alexis, Clara and I stared at him.

"I think Dad has lost the plot," Clara murmured.

"Why have you put Kimmy's food bag in front of us?" Alexis asked.

"Because inside it, you will find" – Mum began, reaching into the food bag and digging  around until she pulled out a small black box with a golden clasp – "the Light of the World."

My jaw dropped to the floor. "You've been keeping the Light of the World in KIMMY'S FOOD BAG?! WHAT WERE YOU THINKING?!"

"It was your father's genius idea," Mum gushed, fluttering her eyelashes at him as he puffed out his chest. "Where else could be safer?"

"Oh, I don't know, maybe an unbreakable vault in an unbreakable bank with an unbreakable security system?" I cried, looking at them as though they were both mad.

"Too obvious." Mum shrugged. "That's where everyone thinks we've been keeping it, no doubt. No one would think we'd stash it in the house and especially not in a dog food bag. Should Mr. Mercury come calling, he'd NEVER think to look there. And besides, the box itself is custom-made by Nanny Beam. You need several codes and a Beam family eye retinal scan to get this thing to open."

"We knew that if anyone approached this dog food bag, Kimmy would go nuts, especially if it was someone other than a family member," Dad pointed out proudly. "You can't touch this bag without Kimmy running straight in here, no matter where she is. She has incredible hearing, as you know."

He patted Kimmy on the head as her tongue lolled out. She remained staring determinedly at the bag in the hope it might open of its own accord if she looked at it long enough.

"That makes her the perfect alarm," Mum added, bending down to give her a neck scratch. Kimmy gave her a slobbery lick and then returned to her mission of staring the dog food bag open.

"You know," Alexis said slowly, "this *almost* makes sense."

"I think it's brilliant," Clara declared with a giggle. "Unexpected and simple."

"Thank you, Clara," Dad said, putting the bag back in its place on the shelf. "I was quite pleased with that brain wave, I must admit."

Mum straightened and pressed the box into my hand. "Here you go, Aurora. It's in your hands now, quite literally. We're here to help, whatever you need."

"Thanks, Mum," I said, clutching the box and nestling into her as she put her arms round me. "I'm not sure I can forgive you for keeping it in a dog food bag, but give it time."

She chuckled. "So, what's the next move?"

I pulled back and turned to Clara. "This is where you come in."

"Reporting for duty," she said, giving me a little salute. "What do you need?"

"We need to get out of the house without the agents noticing."

"We?" she asked, raising her eyebrows.

I nodded. "Aunt Lucinda is going to take me, Cherry and JJ somewhere. Mum and Alexis, I'd like you to come, too, if you don't mind? Alexis, you'll need to bring all the equipment you need for hacking into a security system."

Alexis's eyes brightened and he rubbed his hands together in a mock-evil way. "I'm loving this plan already. I'll get my laptop ready."

Dad groaned as Alexis hurried away. "I don't even WANT to know how many laws my family are about to break in order to save the world."

"That will teach you for marrying a superhero."

Mum grinned, giving him a kiss on the cheek. "Of course I'll come with you, Aurora."

"Great, so Dad, that leaves you and Clara in charge of getting us out of the house and to Aunt Lucinda's car parked around the corner, without any MI5 agents spotting us. We're ready to go when you are." I grimaced as I saw an agent passing by the window of the boot room. "It's not going to be easy. They're everywhere."

Clara let out a long sigh. "Aurora, I recently wrote a chemistry paper on mononuclear and binuclear molybdenum complexes. I THINK I can handle sneaking people out of a house." She looked up at Dad. "I have an idea. It involves filling the entire house with a harmless, luminous green vapor."

"Let's get started," he said, giving me a high five as he followed Clara out of the boot room and up the stairs.

A few minutes later Aunt Lucinda put her foot down on the pedal and we sped down the road away from our house, which currently had green smoke billowing from every crevice. MI5 agents were desperately falling over themselves to get in to see what was going on, completely unaware we'd all sneaked out past them during the chaos.

I laughed as I spotted Clara through her bedroom window, holding what looked like an entire science apparatus with beakers bubbling over, while Dad came out onto the front lawn holding a cup of tea, with the agents in tow, and looking perfectly relaxed as he explained it was just his daughter's science experiment gone awry. Everything was fine and they could go back to their positions guarding the house.

"You OK, Aurora?" Cherry asked, nudging me as I turned around in my seat to face forward.

"Yeah." I grinned. "I'm OK."

One thing this whole superhero thing had really taught me is that, when you're setting off on a new adventure and you don't know what dangers lie ahead, it really helps to have the best family in the world beside you.

14

"Just so I'm clear," Mum said slowly from the front seat, as Lucinda parked the car in front of the prison, "your plan is to break my evil cousin out of jail."

"That's correct."

Mum swiveled to face us in the back. "Seriously?"

"Yup. Seriously." I gave her a stern look. "You *said* you trusted me."

"I know, I do trust you. It's just" – she

hesitated – "we're talking about breaking someone out of a high-security prison here. And not just anyone, but Darek Vermore. He was behind all this chaos in the first place!"

"He also knows exactly where to go underneath the aurora borealis to return the Light of the World to its rightful place," I explained calmly. "If we really want to stop Mr. Mercury, then the most important thing is to make sure the Light of the World is safe. As good as the dog-food-bag hiding place was, it's not where the precious stone belongs."

"What's that about a dog food bag?" Aunt Lucinda asked.

"And you're sure we shouldn't just call Nanny Beam and explain?" Mum said, ignoring her sister. "That way we don't have to break anyone out."

"Mum, there is no chance Nanny Beam will let Darek Vermore walk out of that prison. No, the fewer people who know what's going on, the better."

"There's no fun in him walking out of prison, anyway." JJ grinned next to me. "Much more fun to break him out."

"I can't believe we're about to do this," Cherry said, fiddling with her headphones and checking that they were all in order.

"I can't believe I'm trying to break into a prison security system," Alexis said from the row of seats right at the back of the car. "Which, by the way, is much harder to do when the ostrich sitting next to you isn't letting you have any elbow room."

He glared at Alfred, who was perched next to him, taking up two seats and still wearing all of Dad's ties. He had also added one of Mum's giant sun hats to his outfit.

"How are you getting on?" I asked hopefully.

"OK," Alexis shrugged, peering at his

laptop screen and typing frantically. "It's pretty complicated, but Nanny Beam has taken me through this kind of thing before. I guess she wasn't expecting me to use it against one of her own high-security prisons."

"I guess not," Mum said through gritted teeth, before letting out a long sigh. "Honestly, what a family."

"If it makes you feel any better, Mrs. Beam – sorry, Kiyana – I think your family is the most AWESOME family ever," JJ said enthusiastically. "And I have a dad with super strength and a mum who can walk through walls, so that's really saying something."

"Thank you, JJ." Mum smiled, before glancing nervously at the prison in front of us. "Do you have a plan for breaking Darek out then, Aurora? You can fill us in while Alexis works."

"Yes, good idea," I said. "Cherry and JJ, did you bring the bag from my room?"

"Got it here," Cherry said, holding it up.

"OK, good. It contains a few of Fred's tricks that he's left at the house before. There should be a smoke bomb or two in there."

Cherry zipped open the bag and held them up triumphantly.

"Here's the plan," I began, taking a deep breath. "Mum, you come with me, Cherry, JJ and Alfred into the prison. We say that we're visiting Darek—"

"Aren't there visiting hours you're supposed to stick to?" Mum pointed out.

"Yes, but I'm Lightning Girl and you're *you*, so I'm guessing we can persuade them to let us talk to him about an urgent matter that's just come up," I replied confidently. "Once we're in with him, Cherry will be using her supersonic hearing to listen out for anyone coming, and JJ will be on hand with his super strength if anything goes wrong."

"My karate skills are outrageously good, so don't worry, people, you're all in safe hands," JJ declared.

"Yeah," Cherry said, sighing dramatically, "because I'm sure Mrs. Beam, a superhero who has been saving the world for years, really needs your help in a jam."

JJ frowned at her.

"Once we're with Darek, Alexis will cut out the security system," I continued, "meaning all alarms will go down. We let off one of Fred's smoke bombs and in all the confusion we smuggle Darek out hidden in Alfred's feathers and head to where Aunt Lucinda is waiting with the engine on for a speedy getaway. Job done."

Mum blinked at me. "We smuggle him out hidden in Alfred's *feathers*?"

"It's the best I could come up with at short notice, and with all the confusion, I think it has a good chance of working," I insisted, sounding a lot more confident than I felt.

"OR I could just use the blaster that is built into this amazing supercar to blow a big hole in the wall of Darek's cell. We get him out and off we go, flying into the distance," Aunt Lucinda suggested. "Much easier."

"That sounds so cool!" JJ exclaimed, his eyes widening as Aunt Lucinda pointed at a big red button. "Let's go with that idea."

I shook my head. "No. We're already breaking out a prisoner; let's not cause as much damage as possible along the way."

"I agree," Mum said, giving Aunt Lucinda a stern look.

"Always the sensible one, Kiyana," Aunt Lucinda said to Mum, drawing her finger away from the big red button. "When are you going to let yourself have a little bit of fun?"

"Oh, and your idea of having fun is shooting

a blaster out of a car?"

"Yes, I think that sounds like a LOT of fun."

"That's so like you, Lucinda: never thinking of consequences, just pressing big red buttons throughout life and then leaving all of us to clear up the mess," Mum mumbled. "Just like that time with the castle."

"I KNEW you were going to bring that up," Aunt Lucinda huffed. "You always have to throw that in my face!"

"You knocked over that entire toy-brick castle and you knew I'd been working on it for weeks! You didn't even care!"

"We were six years old and I didn't knock it over on purpose! You shouldn't have built it in our bedroom when you KNEW that's where I practiced spinning round as fast as possible until I got so dizzy I fell over!"

"Yeah, well YOU—"

"That's enough!" I cried, leaning forward to address them both. "We need to work together, remember? Otherwise we don't have a chance of pulling this off."

"Fine," Mum said through gritted teeth, narrowing her eyes at her twin sister. "But you had better behave, Lucinda."

"Cross my heart, Kiyana," Aunt Lucinda

said, sticking her tongue out at her.

"I'm in!" Alexis announced suddenly, causing everyone to turn to look at him. "I did it. I can shut it down, but it's only going to be for a few seconds. You'll have to act fast."

"Nice!" JJ high-fived him. "Does that mean it's time to go?"

"It does." I gulped. "Everyone ready?"

Cherry smiled at me encouragingly and opened the car door. "After you, Lightning Girl."

"Good luck!" Aunt Lucinda called out after us, as we made our way through the parking lot. "Loving the hat, Alfred, darling!"

Walking through the prison doors with Cherry, JJ, Mum and Alfred in tow, I tried to act as naturally as possible. I strolled up to the reception and cleared my throat.

"We're here to visit Darek Vermore," I told the prison guard behind the screen.

He looked shocked at the group suddenly before him, his eyes lingering suspiciously on Alfred for a few moments.

"All of you?" he said eventually.

"Yes, all of us. We have some questions of the utmost importance for him. Something has just come up and uh ... we need to speak to him. So, yeah, shall I fill in the visitors' book?"

My voice had gone slightly more high-pitched than normal and I could tell that the prison officer wasn't completely convinced. He opened his mouth to say something but before he could, Mum stepped forward to put her hand on my shoulder.

"It's a matter of national security; I'm sure you understand," Mum said coolly. "My name is Kiyana Beam and if you're in any way hesitant about the nature of our visit, please do feel free to call Patricia Beam of MI5. She'll be happy to confirm the necessity of our seeing Darek

Vermore and we don't mind waiting."

I looked up at Mum as though she was MAD, but she must have done this kind of thing before because the prison officer immediately slid some passes to us and shook his head, beads of sweat breaking out on his forehead.

"No ... no need to put in a call to Agent Beam, ma'am; you go on ahead," he stammered.

He gestured for another prison officer to take us through and I leaned into Mum as we passed through the many heavy doors to the interview room.

"*How?*" I asked.

Mum smiled mischievously. "She may be Nanny Beam to you, but to everyone else she's Patricia Beam, Head of MI5 and someone you do NOT want to mess with. Ever since she told me what she really does, I've discovered that it can be handy to drop her job into certain conversations from time to time."

"I'll remember that."

We waited in the interview room in silence until Darek was brought in. He looked confused to see us all in there and then stopped in his tracks when he saw that Mum was among the group, his expression becoming fearful.

"Hello, Darek. Have a seat. We have a few questions for you." Mum smiled warmly at the prison guard who had brought him in. "We can take it from here."

The guard nodded and scuttled out of the room, shutting the door behind him.

"OK, Cherry, headphones on. Everyone ready?" I said hurriedly, as Cherry followed my instructions.

Mum sent Alexis a message and Alfred stalked over to Darek, pecked him with his beak until he stood up and then shoved him under his wing.

"Hey!" Darek cried, his voice muffled

through the feathers. "What's going on?"

Suddenly, the lights all went off and JJ, who was standing at the door peering out of the window, spoke in the darkness of the room.

"OK, all the red lights above the doors down the corridor have gone green."

"The panic is starting," Cherry whispered to us. "I can hear the prison guards. We need to move fast."

I concentrated as hard as possible, which wasn't easy considering how nervous I was feeling, and let the warm tingling feeling run down through my arms. My fingers sparked and then my hands gave out a warm glow, lighting our way.

"Let's go!" I said, throwing open the door. "JJ, smoke bombs now!"

JJ let off the smoke bombs in the corridor which sparked immediate chaos. I really thought the plan was working until something

happened that I hadn't exactly thought through: the smoke faded. And Alexis had managed to shut down the lights and alarm system, but clearly they had a backup system in place.

We'd just reached the first door to get through in the corridor when everything came back up and running. The strip lighting switched on, bathing us in harsh artificial light, and the doors locked, stopping us in our tracks. The smoke bombs had worn off.

"Uh-oh..." Cherry whispered, lowering her headphones back round her neck, noting the prison guards turning their attention to us.

As their expressions changed from confusion to anger, I guessed they had cottoned on to what was happening. They slowly surrounded us and we all put our hands up, retreating into the interview room.

"Please tell me this wasn't the entirety of your plan to get me out of here," Darek mumbled, poking his head up through Alfred's feathers. Alfred accidentally on purpose stomped on his foot in reply and Darek cried out in pain.

"What do we do?" Cherry whispered, shuffling backward and knocking into a chair.

"We can take them," JJ said determinedly. "Just give me the signal, Lightning Girl, and I'll start with a high kick."

My head racing as I desperately tried to think up a plan B, there was suddenly a loud beeping horn from outside and then the unmistakable sound of a supercar revving.

"Here we go," Mum muttered before crying out, "Everyone away from the wall!"

Just as we darted to the sides of the room and crouched down, there was a huge **CRASH**. I looked up to see a gaping hole in the wall behind us and Aunt Lucinda waving at us through the front window of the car.

"Yoo-hoo!" She grinned, revving the engine again. "Anyone need a ride?"

Before the prison guards knew what was going on, Mum grabbed Darek by the scruff of his neck and dragged him through the hole in the wall and toward the car, the rest of us racing after her.

A couple of guards who were quick off the mark yelled at us to stop and attempted to launch through the wall, but Alfred was prepared and blocked them with his bottom, sending them flying backward as they crashed blindly into his feathers.

We clambered into the car and once Alfred was in, we slammed the door behind him and Aunt Lucinda set off.

"Seat belts on, please!" she instructed, calmly putting her sunglasses on while the rest of us scrambled into a seat and buckled in. Wings sprang out of the sides of the car.

That familiar robotic voice rang out of the car's speakers – "Flight mode engaged. Prepare for takeoff" – and the car began to lift off the ground, soaring upward into the air.

"Now, THAT is how you break out of prison," Aunt Lucinda said with a smug smile at Mum, as she glanced down at the prison guards on the ground who were becoming little dots in the distance. She caught Darek's eye in the rearview mirror. "Hello, evil cousin. How unpleasant to see you again."

"Thank you for breaking me out," Darek replied, looking about him. "I see you've remodeled. Nanny Beam never told me she was working on a new flying car. It's very impressive."

"Don't touch anything," Aunt Lucinda said, narrowing her eyes at him. "Now, Aurora, to where exactly am I flying this merry crew?"

I turned to Darek. "We had a deal. I break you out of prison, you help us return the Light of the World."

"Well then, Darek?" Mum asked from the front seat, refusing to look at him. "Where are we going?"

"Iceland," he replied, gazing out of the window at the clouds. "We're going to Iceland."

The video call screen in the car started flashing green and the robotic voice announced, "Incoming call: Mummy."

"Uh-oh," Aunt Lucinda whispered, before saying clearly, "Reject."

The robotic voice replied: "Rejection of call from Mummy overruled."

Nanny Beam's face popped up on the screen and she did NOT look pleased. Two of her agents were standing behind her, including the agent who had been so nice to me that time at the bowling alley when I thought it was a haunted house. She was grimacing behind Nanny Beam's back before Nanny Beam had even said anything, so I knew we were in big trouble.

"How did you overrule my rejection of the call?" Aunt Lucinda gasped. "You didn't tell me about that feature."

"We can discuss that another time, Lucinda," Nanny Beam snapped. "I want to know just WHY you have broken DAREK out of PRISON?!"

"We can explain—" Mum began.

"Tell me where you are right this minute!"

"Nanny Beam," I began, "we have to go to—"

"Are you out of your minds?" Nanny Beam cried, throwing her hands up in the air. "You BROKE HIM OUT OF PRISON!"

"It's for good reason," Mum said, wincing at Nanny Beam's tone.

"If you don't tell me where you are, I'm going to track the car and come to get you."

"Actually, Mummy, don't be mad," Aunt Lucinda said, before taking a deep breath, "but Alfred ripped out the tracker last week. He took the car for a spin, you see, and when he discovered that I'd known where he was the whole time, he was very angry. He thought it was an invasion of privacy. So, he took the tracker out and threw it into the Thames."

"We need Darek," Mum said sternly. "You're going to have to trust us."

Nanny Beam shut her eyes in despair. The nice agent from the bowling alley suddenly cleared her throat and took a small step forward.

"Boss," she said nervously, "you're getting another call."

"Ah, well, off you go, Mummy, lovely to talk to you!" Aunt Lucinda said. "We'll be in touch soon! Toodle-loo!"

She quickly hung up on Nanny Beam.

"Well," she said, smiling at us in the rearview mirror, "I think that went as well as it could, don't you? If we get in trouble for this, Kiyana, I'm blaming you. You owe me for that time I took all the heat about the broken window when we were ten years old. I haven't forgotten that debt."

"You took the heat for that one because YOU were the one who broke the window," Mum said through gritted teeth.

When the car landed in Iceland, it was almost completely dark except for a flickering glow of the northern lights above us.

Darek had directed Aunt Lucinda to stop in the middle of a vast, empty, ice-covered landscape of fields with a swirling river running through it. It felt like there was no one for miles. It was so peaceful. Aunt Lucinda switched off the engine and, pulling my coat tightly round me, I stepped out and gazed up at the sky.

"Whoa," JJ said, coming to stand next to me and looking up in awe at the beautiful array of green and purple lights swirled through the sky. "Is that the northern lights? I've only ever seen pictures before."

"It is," Mum said, holding Darek firmly by the arm as Aunt Lucinda flanked his other side. "But the northern lights don't usually flicker."

"The aurora is fading," Aunt Lucinda said softly, shaking her head. "Something's not right."

Cherry leaned against the car. "Aurora, is this all connected to the Light of the World somehow? Mr. Mercury stealing things and kidnapping people?"

"Once we get the Light of the World to where it belongs, everything will be better," I said firmly, carefully avoiding her question.

"Cherry, can you and Alfred stay with the car? Just in case."

"Of course," she nodded, glancing at Alfred who had put on some earmuffs.

I made sure Darek was out of earshot and then leaned toward her to whisper in her ear.

"The button there on the dashboard" – I pointed to a purple button with a swirled symbol on it – "is a direct line to Nanny Beam. Listen out and if you hear us getting into trouble, press that and call her to come here straightaway, OK? Just in case Darek tries to pull something."

"Got it, Lightning Girl," she said, tapping her headphones. "I'll be listening to you the whole time. You won't be alone."

"You stay here, darling," Aunt Lucinda told Alfred, who looked offended at the suggestion. "Now, now, don't get cross. It's nothing personal, we just need someone to stay behind who can drive the car just in case."

"Wait, what?" Cherry said, insulted. "You trust an OSTRICH to drive, over me?"

Alfred glared at her with his beady eye and she recoiled under his glare.

"OK, OK," she said hurriedly. "If anything happens you're the driver."

"If he gets impatient, then there are sweets in the car," Aunt Lucinda informed her, giving Alfred a pat on his feathers. "Whatever you do, don't eat any yourself. I once nabbed a raspberry one when I thought he wasn't looking." She grimaced. "When he was finished sulking, he threw everything in my house outside the window into a big pile on the front lawn. And when I say everything, I mean, *everything*. Even the bathtub."

"Um, OK," Cherry said, staring at Alfred who had found a telescope in the car and was now pushing it toward Cherry to set up for him. "That doesn't sound like an overreaction."

"Darek, lead the way," I instructed, shoving my hands in my coat pockets. I clutched my fingers round the box containing the Light of the World. I wasn't going to let it go until it was safely back where it belonged.

Darek nodded ahead of him. "It's that way. Any chance I can have these handcuffs taken off now?"

"No chance," Mum replied, gripping his arm even tighter. "We're not taking any risks with you, Darek."

"I've tried to tell you how much I regret—"

"Nice try," Aunt Lucinda interrupted, prodding him in the back with her manicured fingernail. "We don't want your apologies. Start walking."

JJ and I followed behind as the three of them led the way. We walked in silence for a bit and I took the time to think about what a momentous occasion this really was. Everything had been so rushed and complicated up until this moment that it was nice to walk in silence in the crisp, cold air. I knew I was doing the right thing, but part of me felt a little sad that I wouldn't have the Light of the World near me after today. I felt so connected to it.

"Hey, Darek," JJ suddenly said, breaking the silence, "how come you know exactly where to return the precious stone?"

"I have studied the precious stones all my life."

I instantly tensed at his mentioning more than one precious stone, but luckily I didn't think anyone else noticed.

"If that's true, then how come you messed up transferring Aurora's powers to you?" JJ asked.

Darek stopped in his tracks to look down his nose at JJ. "Excuse me?"

"You tried to steal Aurora's powers, right?

But it didn't work. If you know everything there is to know about the precious stone, how did you get that wrong?"

"He has a point, Darek," Aunt Lucinda grinned, enjoying Darek's embarrassment. "Quite a big mistake really."

Darek pursed his lips in irritation and pushed on, Mum holding his arm in her strong grip.

"I didn't realize that you needed a *specific* natural light, the aurora borealis, overhead to transfer the powers," he explained reluctantly. "Everything about the Light of the World was myths and legends. Folktales passed down to generations by mouth. Not everything was explained clearly and it was difficult to know what to believe and which bits were just made up."

"But you didn't know how to transfer the powers, even though you'd dedicated your whole life to it," JJ added breezily. "Aurora figured it out by reading that book. And she's only twelve years old."

Aunt Lucinda sniggered and Darek looked as though his head might explode.

"I didn't realize that book had such valuable information in it," Darek seethed, staring straight ahead and refusing to look at JJ, who had now fallen into step alongside them. "If I had, obviously I would have consulted it earlier."

As they talked, I started to get a strange feeling. It came on so gradually, I didn't even notice it was happening until my fingers started tingling and I realized that I felt really warm, even though it was cold out, and the anxiety I'd felt about our mission had completely faded to a sense that everything was going to be all right. It was like there was a light shining within me.

The closer we got to a striking, distinct

mountain right in the middle of the vast, empty landscape and underneath the northern lights, the more the feeling grew and grew. I slowed my steps.

"Wait," I called out, causing everyone to stop and turn around.

"Aurora, what are you doing hanging back there?" Mum asked, gesturing for me to catch up.

"Darek, do we need to go this way?" I asked, pointing to the mountain.

Darek snorted. "What, up Kirkjufell Mountain? No, we are not going that way."

"But . . . I feel drawn to it."

"OK, well, still, that's not where the Light of the World belongs," Darek insisted. "It belongs in the direction we're heading now."

"Are you sure?" I asked, looking down at my hands as the warm tingling feeling ran through them, like the sparks were dancing about inside my veins.

Mum looked at him suspiciously and he held up his hands defensively.

"Look, if you don't trust me then we can go up Kirkjufell Mountain so you can be sure, but you can't go up there without a local guide as it can be a dangerous trek if you don't know where to go. We'd have to go to the nearest town and ask for someone to take us." He sighed. "It's up to you. You're just wasting time, but hey, from my point of view, traipsing pointlessly around a mountain is still better than being in that prison, so really, I'm happy either way."

"What do you want to do, Aurora?" Mum asked.

I shook my head. This was too important a task for me to just decide to go somewhere on a whim because I had a warm feeling. I had to be responsible about it. The mountain path didn't exactly look easy and whatever else Darek said, he was right about needing a local guide. We'd already gotten this far; it was too much of a risk to change the plan now.

"Let's keep going," I said, hurrying to catch up.

We continued and the feeling began to fade until we were far enough of a distance away for me to go back to being cold again.

"Everything all right, Aurora?" JJ asked, walking alongside me. "Are you feeling nervous?"

"I don't know," I said in a low voice, watching Darek's back. "Something doesn't feel right. Why did I feel drawn to that place if the Light of the World is supposed to be somewhere else? I feel cold and empty here and Darek says we're getting close."

JJ raised his eyebrows. "You think he's fooling us? Surely he wouldn't be so silly. There's one of him and four of us; we all have superpowers and he doesn't."

"Yeah, that's true," I said. "Still, something doesn't—"

"Here we are!" Darek announced eagerly, stopping suddenly. "There, straight ahead."

In front of us was a towering jumble of large rocks, in the middle of which was a gap just big enough for someone to squeeze through.

"That's it?" Aunt Lucinda said in disbelief. "I hope you're not expecting us to crawl into that gap. It's absolutely out of the question. These clothes are NOT machine washable and it looks like a rather tight squeeze."

I stepped round him to approach the rocks cautiously. "What's in there?"

"A tunnel," Darek answered.

"Does the tunnel go underground?" JJ asked. Darek nodded in reply. "Just like in Cherry's vision!"

"What vision?" Mum asked.

"I don't think this is the right place," I said, peering into the darkness of the space between the rocks. "Let's go back to Kirkjufell Mountain."

"I'm afraid that's not possible," Darek replied, the corners of his mouth twitching into a smirk.

Suddenly, JJ cried out as he was pounced on

by several guards who seemed to come out of nowhere. Mum gasped and turned to help him, facing her palms upward and shooting out light beams with great energy force, but just as she did so, more guards appeared from behind the rocks, pinning her and Aunt Lucinda to the ground.

"You'll have to make do without your light powers, Beams," Darek said, watching as the guards struggled to put some kind of specially designed gloves on Mum and Aunt Lucinda's hands. "These gloves have been created with you in mind. I know how you love bespoke designs, Lucinda, and they are exclusive to Vermore Enterprises. Be careful with that one," he yelled to the many guards holding JJ to the ground, "he has super strength. A little sedation once we're underground might be in order."

He raised his eyes to meet mine and I stumbled backward, swallowing the lump in my throat and desperately trying to get my powers flowing. But as I retreated, someone's large hands gripped round my arms and yanked my hands behind my back.

I cried out in pain as they held my arms there and then tied them together, before putting a pair of gloves on – the kind that were keeping Mum and Aunt Lucinda's powers in check. I tried to wrestle out of the person's grip, but it was no use.

"Hello, Aurora," a familiar voice said in my ear.

He spun me round and I stood face-to-face with Mr. Mercury.

"You tracked me down in the end, congratulations." He let out a loud, piercing

cackle before dragging me toward the tunnel. "Come on, Beams. Let's go for a little walk."

Still struggling against his grip, I managed to whisper, "Cherry, time to press that button," before I was gruffly pushed through the rocks and led on into the darkness.

Mr. Mercury walked just ahead of me, holding a low-light flashlight. Once we were through the entrance to the tunnel, it got slightly bigger so that we didn't have to crouch or duck our heads walking through it.

"Are you all right, Aurora?" Mum called out a few feet behind me. "Are you hurt?"

"She's fine," Darek growled. "Just walk."

We could barely see anything, but after a few paces I could make out bars of a prison cell built into one side of the tunnel with a small light hanging from the ceiling. I gasped as I peered through the bars on my way past. The pope and the Dalai Lama were sitting together in there on the cold, damp ground.

"LET THEM GO!" I yelled, trying to struggle out of Darek's grip.

"Now, now, Lightning Girl," he sneered in my ear as he pushed me on through the tunnel, "they're just fine. You keep walking."

"We're going to get you out of here," I heard Mum say firmly as she walked past them behind me. "I promise."

I don't know if it's because she's been a superhero for so many years, but Mum has a way of saying stuff like that so calmly and confidently, you can't help but believe her.

We continued along the rough passageway and I heard a clatter and then an "Ouch!" from JJ behind me as he stumbled over the uneven floor.

"Keep walking," one of the guards barked at him.

"It would be easier if I could actually see where I was going," JJ pointed out.

"Try doing this in heels," Aunt Lucinda grumbled. "Really, can't we have some more light?"

"No," snapped Darek, gripping my right arm and dragging me forward any time I slowed. "Although I'm surprised you're still bothering with that flashlight, Desmond. I would have thought you'd have gotten around to installing some lights in here by now."

Even in the dim light from the flashlight, I could see Mr. Mercury's whole body tense at the use of his name.

"*Don't* call me that," he hissed.

"What? Desmond?" Darek replied innocently. "Desmond Silicon? But that's your name, isn't it?"

"You know how I feel about that name!" Mr. Mercury spat. "So, shut it!"

"Oh yes, you don't like it because it reminds you of how much you've let down your dear old mother, Mrs. Silicon," Darek said gleefully. "I wonder how she'd feel if she found out her darling Desmond kidnapped the pope and the Dalai Lama? I don't think she'd be too proud of you, and she'd probably love your sister, the successful one, even *more*."

"I said, *shut it*."

The conversation was confusing me. Mr. Mercury worked for Darek, didn't he? But he wasn't acting as though he was talking to his boss. Surely he should be afraid of Darek, the powerful mastermind behind everything, but instead, he was acting as though they were on an equal footing. And I knew it couldn't be the other way round, and that Darek worked for Mr. Mercury – it was obvious just from this conversation that they had no respect for one another.

What was going on?

"I would come down from that high horse, if I were you, Vermore." Mr. Mercury sniggered. "You're not exactly in anyone's good books."

"What do you mean?" Darek replied hurriedly, his voice tense. "I've brought the girl, haven't I?"

"You think that will make up for everything you've done?" Mr. Mercury snorted as the tunnel curved to the left. "You've got a lot of begging to do and I doubt forgiveness is in the cards."

"But I've achieved more than *you* ever could," Darek squeaked, his hand gripping my arm even tighter, as though he was afraid I might escape his clutches, even though I had nowhere to run.

"You're lucky we were able to set up the trap

for your arrival. How were you planning on letting us know that you were on your way here with Lightning Girl?" Mr. Mercury asked.

"I knew *she* would get a message to you once I was broken out. I wasn't worried. She's not like her *useless brother*."

Mr. Mercury frowned at him.

"Wait," I said, tripping forward, "your sister, Selena Silicon, is involved in this? *How*? Darek, you haven't spoken to anyone since we broke you out of prison. How could she get a message to anyone?"

"Enough talk from you," Mr. Mercury spat. "Anyway, Vermore, what makes you think that what you've done now is enough to make up for what you did?"

"But ... b-bringing L-Lightning Girl must count for s-something?" Darek replied.

I'd never heard Darek talk like this before. His voice tremored as he spoke and I could hear him swallowing nervously. Even his hand began shaking slightly. Who was he so afraid of? And what had he done to be so worried?

"I suppose it may count for *something*," Mr. Mercury said breezily, clearly enjoying torturing him. "But what you did was a great betrayal. And it will be VERY difficult to forget that."

"It was a moment's misjudgment," Darek snapped loudly, his voice echoing down the tunnel. "I made ONE mistake. I got carried away. I wasn't thinking! I just—"

"Save it," Mr. Mercury interrupted as we finally got to the end of a tunnel, stopping in front of the heavy metal door. "I'm not the one you need to be groveling to, Vermore."

Darek gulped.

Mr. Mercury turned around, shining the flashlight right in my eyes. I squinted as he held it up to my face.

"There's no way you're getting out of this one, Lightning Girl," he said with a victorious smirk that made my blood boil. "In the end, after all our encounters, I have won and you have lost."

"I don't know if it counts as winning when along the way you get ants down your pants," I muttered, recalling the time Fred shoved his red ant farm down Mr. Mercury's trousers in the Natural History Museum. "And you've been sat on by an ostrich. Twice."

Several of the guards burst out laughing and Mr. Mercury was so angry, it looked as though his head might explode.

"Oi! Shut it!" he yelled at the guards, all of whom fell silent immediately.

"Yes, my dear ostrich, Alfred, really doesn't like you, does he? I can't think why when you're so ... charming," Aunt Lucinda mused, setting off the guards again who couldn't stop giggling.

"Why don't we just go in?" Darek suggested through gritted teeth as Mr. Mercury's face completely scrunched up in frustration. "I think it's time. You can taunt Lightning Girl later, if you wish, but I hardly think we should keep anyone waiting any longer."

Mr. Mercury spun round and shone the flashlight beam at the keypad next to the door. He punched in a long code and then had his eye retina scanned, as well as voice activation. The door clunked as it automatically unlocked, and Mr. Mercury pressed his whole body weight against it and pushed it open.

I thought that wherever we were walking into might be better lit than the tunnel, but I was wrong. It was obvious we were in some kind of underground lair, but it was badly lit by only a few hazy blue floor lights in various spots in the room. I could just make out some impressive-looking machinery in the corner of the room and a variety of computer screens dotted around the wall. From the dull glow of a floor light in another corner, I saw a comfortable chair with a pile of books stacked next to it.

"Where are we?" I asked, squinting through the darkness. "What is this place?"

"It smells awful," Aunt Lucinda pointed out. "This place could really do with some scented candles. I could give you a list of some lovely brands, if you'd like, Darek. A couple of diffusers here and there, and even an underground lair could be transformed into a home!"

"This isn't my home," Darek replied.

"No," came a low, cold voice that made a shiver run down my spine, "it's mine."

I heard a ripple of gasps at the hidden voice from the corner of the room. I wished I could use my powers to light up the room and my fingers itched in the gloves behind my back.

"Who are you?" Mum asked angrily, with no giveaway of fear in her voice. She really was the bravest person in the world. "What do you want?"

The mysterious owner of the voice stepped forward and I could see that there was a hood covering their face, just like in Cherry's vision.

"I was hoping to meet you, Lightning Girl," the hooded figure said slowly, approaching me. From his voice it was clear that he was a man, but I didn't recognize it.

As he came closer, Mr. Mercury quickly shut off his flashlight, but just before he did, I managed to catch a glimpse of the figure's hand. It was horribly scarred and the skin sunken, covered in what looked like patterns of dark ink, as though the tendons and veins in his hand were outlined by black marker.

I felt strange as he got closer, like my powers were rebelling inside, desperate for the warm light to burst and shine out in protest of his presence. He stopped about three feet from me, his face completely covered by the hood so that even as my eyes slowly got used to the dark, I still couldn't see who he was.

"Well done for bringing her here, Darek," he said eventually, but he didn't sound all that pleased. "*Something* you've done right."

"I... I wanted to say s ... sorry," Darek stammered, his fingers shaking against my arm, "about everything. I tried to get a message to you—"

"I got your messages," the figure hissed.

"If ... if you'd just let me explain," Darek began.

"Your actions seem a little ungrateful, Darek," he said calmly. "Trying to take Aurora's powers for yourself. Everything was going perfectly to plan. You had Aurora, you had the Light of the World, you'd booked your travel here. I must say, at that point I was impressed that you'd really managed to pull it off." He let out a long sigh. "And then you made a hasty decision to betray everything we'd worked for. Pity for you it didn't pay off."

"I got caught up in the moment. I was always going to—"

"Excuses, excuses," the voice whispered from beneath the hood. "I hope you didn't think that you'd win back my favor by merely bringing her here."

"N-no, of course not," Darek whimpered. "I just—"

"If anyone should take credit, it should be Silicon over there. Aurora, you made the decision to come all this way because of the panic Silicon was causing by kidnapping public figures, isn't that right? That will always be the weakness of superheroes. So predictable by always trying to do the right thing."

"Let the pope and the Dalai Lama go," I demanded, wriggling against Darek's shaky grip.

"I'm not going to hurt them. They were only ever a distraction. I wanted the precious stones, but I didn't need the guardians," the hooded man sneered, his voice turning sour. "You see, Aurora Beam, you were the only guardian I really wanted, but I knew that if I were to cause a little panic, then your dear Nanny Beam would put all her efforts and resources into protecting the Queen, and in the meantime, our little guardian of the Light of the World would start to listen to the suggestion that the only way to keep your precious stone truly safe would be to return it to the aurora borealis." He stopped to laugh maliciously. "Clever, don't you think? Not only did I get the other precious stones, but you brought the last one to me of your own accord."

"Other precious stones?" Aunt Lucinda said. "What other precious stones?"

"*Who are you?*" I asked, peering at him.

"Haven't you worked it out yet?" He sighed. "Did you really think that *Darek* could be behind all this? Did you honestly believe that my incompetent *son* was the genius behind everything I've achieved?"

My insides seemed to turn to ice and I felt as though my breath had been knocked out of me. At first I let his words hang in the stunned silence and then I found the strength to speak.

"Your . . . *son*?" I whispered.

"Yes, my son. It's a pleasure to meet you at last, Aurora Beam," he spoke into the darkness. "I'm your long-dead great-uncle Nolan."

17

"That's not possible," I said, my shaky voice cutting through the shocked silence of the dark cave. "You're dead. You've been dead for years. You were killed!"

"Almost," he corrected me. "But not quite."

"The explosion of light in the warehouse. It killed you."

"That's what I led everyone to believe."

"Come into the light," Mum croaked. "Why should we believe you? Our Uncle Nolan is dead."

"You shouldn't believe everything your mother tells you," he sneered at Mum. "Fooling my sister into thinking I was dead was easier than I thought. I suppose she wanted to believe it, which made the whole thing a lot smoother. The day of the warehouse explosion, I wasn't killed. But I was almost destroyed."

He moved away as he spoke, carefully avoiding the few spots of faint light. There was a sound of a drawer opening, some paper rustling and as he came closer again, he was holding an old newspaper article. I didn't have to see it to know which one it was. The same one I'd found in Nanny Beam's house last summer, detailing the tragic event.

"I don't remember much," he said, straightening the article. "The details are all a bit hazy. That day, everything changed."

"*Why?*" Mum said, and it sounded like she was crying. "Why would you do that to your sister? Make her believe you were dead when you weren't?"

"There are advantages to being dead," he said simply, letting the newspaper article go and flutter to the floor. "People stop looking for you."

"You've been behind everything, then," I said slowly, as I tried to make sense of my jumbled brain. "Not Darek. Why have you been hidden away here?"

There was silence as he inhaled deeply.

"As you already know," he began, "the light explosion in the warehouse all those years ago was caused by one of my less-genius ideas: to extract the powers from the Jewel of Truth and Nobility and transfer those powers to myself."

"What is the Jewel of Truth and Nobility?" Aunt Lucinda asked. "What are you talking about?"

"I do beg your pardon; I forgot it was all

a big secret." He chuckled, clearly enjoying having an audience. "The Light of the World isn't the only precious stone with powers. There are four."

"*Four*," Aunt Lucinda repeated. "Kiyana—"

"It's true," Mum confirmed resentfully.

"Yes. So many family secrets coming out now," he sneered. "But the Jewel of Truth and Nobility turned out to be my downfall. Finally, I had one of the precious stones. And what did I do? I messed it all up and nearly killed myself. My plan backfired."

"The scars and dark marks on your hand. . ." I said.

He looked in my direction, and although I couldn't see his face, I could feel his eyes boring into me. My hands began to burn inside the gloves as my powers of light desperately tried to counteract the darkness and show themselves.

"There was a . . . legend about the stones.

A very old legend that I discovered," he said quietly, as though it pained him to speak about it. "That they were protected, as it were."

"By the guardians."

"Not exactly. I thought it was a silly warning; just a folktale to keep everyone away from them. The powers within the stone protected themselves." He hesitated. "A curse."

"The Jewel of Truth and Nobility . . . cursed you?" I gasped.

"A darkness was embedded into my skin," he snapped. "I haven't been able to go into the light for years. It's too painful; it feels like the light is burning me."

"Like a vampire," JJ pointed out in awe.

"No, not like a *vampire*," Nolan spat in anger. If it wasn't such a serious situation, I would have laughed.

"I don't believe you," I stated. "You must be able to go into the light. Otherwise, how could you have visited Darek in prison?"

Nolan snorted. "You think I'd waste my precious time visiting *him*?"

Darek recoiled next to me.

"I assure you, Lightning Girl, I'm telling the truth," Nolan said. "The precious stone protected itself by cursing me with a darkness. I had to retreat here where there is never much daylight. Luckily, I still had some loyal workers. The Silicons and my son... Well, I say loyal, but I suppose some things change." As he spoke, Darek whimpered. "Darek took over the empire I had built and helped set me up here in Iceland. I had to get away from the world and rebuild my strength. The darkness ... it's..."

His sentence fizzled out and after a few moments, he spoke again so quietly I could barely hear him.

"It's destroying me."

"That's why you need the Light of the World. You think it's going to save you with its powers of light. As though it could turn back time somehow," I said, trying to sound braver than I felt. "Is that really what you think?"

"It won't just save me, Aurora. It will make me the most powerful man in the world," he explained eagerly, almost forgetting himself and coming toward me before he remembered and recoiled again. "I'm connected to these stones now."

"Only the guardians are connected to their stones," I told him firmly. "And only the Beam women have the powers of light."

"No, no, no," he said, becoming more animated as he explained. "The day that darkness got into my skin, it connected me with the powers of the stones. Haven't you seen what's been happening to the world with the precious stones in my power? When

Silicon – or Mr. Mercury to you – brought me the Jewel of Truth and Nobility, I knew that something would happen, but it was better than I'd ever hoped... *The world began to grow darker.*"

He moved toward the computer equipment and typed in something on a keypad, before darting back as all the screens lit up. Each screen showed a different news article from around the world before flicking to the next one, each report detailing a region or country where the light had faded.

"I felt stronger than I'd ever felt with that stone in my grasp," Nolan continued as we all stared up at the screens, "and while I grew stronger, the world grew weaker. The precious stones have more power than you can imagine and it would seem that when they are under my control, connected to my darkness, it strips the light from the world. With all four in my hands, not only would the world tumble into darkness, but I'd be the most powerful man on the planet. I'd have more power than even my sister."

"You've done all this because you're jealous of Nanny Beam," I said, shaking my head. "You never got over that she had powers of light and you didn't."

"I have to say, I hadn't fully worked out my plan right from the start," he said, ignoring my accusation. "Darek shared my love of the precious stones from a young age and agreed that we couldn't let the Beam women take all the powers for themselves. As I've mentioned, after the light explosion, he helped me to retreat here and I instructed him to gain Patricia's trust. I knew that I would one day have my revenge and an inside man would be key to it. Darek began working alongside Patricia and MI5, while I spent years in isolation, recovering and plotting. Learning everything I could about the precious stones and where they were."

"You knew that the Queen had the Jewel of Truth and Nobility. Why didn't you go after it again when you already knew where it was?" I asked.

"A question Darek asked me plenty of times," Nolan replied. "But I knew it would be wise to bide my time. I had to wait until their guard was down to take what was rightfully mine. The only problem was how."

"The Jewel of Truth and Nobility is rightfully the Queen's!"

"It's mine now!" he thundered. He took a moment to collect himself and continued in a calmer voice. "In the end, Darek's betrayal provided the answer to everything, quite out of the blue. The plan had originally been to bring you and the precious stone to me but, at the last minute, when he worked out how to harness the powers of the Light of the World using you, Aurora, he decided to try to get your powers for himself."

I remembered Alexis's confusion over why Darek would secretly organize a private plane to Iceland and then, right before he was due to go, attempt to take my powers.

At Nolan's explanation of his actions, Darek had loosened his grip on my arm and cowered slightly behind me.

"I'm s . . . sorry, Dad," he mumbled.

"His vanity and weakness landed him in prison," Nolan said matter-of-factly, ignoring Darek's apology. "I was disappointed at the betrayal of my son. After all these years under my guidance and knowing the possibility that I might waste away from the darkness in my blood, he felt he was more deserving of the precious stone's powers." Darek cowered even farther behind me and let out a small, barely audible whimper. "But the best thing about it was that Patricia and the Queen thought they'd gotten the culprit who was after the precious stones."

"It was the perfect time for me to strike!" Mr. Mercury interjected with a low cackle. "I had been working in Buckingham Palace for ages in disguise, biding my time and—"

"Yes, thank you, Silicon," Nolan interrupted coldly. "I'll relate my own story if that's all right with you?"

I saw Mr. Mercury's shadow duck at the sharpness of his boss's tone.

"As Silicon mentioned, I'd placed him in Buckingham Palace after his stint at the Superhero Conference, ready to take the Jewel of Truth and Nobility when the time was right. Darek's intentions being discovered led to just that – the presentation of medals to the brave Bright Sparks." Nolan snorted and I saw his hood move as he shook his head in disbelief. "It couldn't be more perfect. The Queen needed the stone in the crown present at the ceremony and ready to be on display so that she could show it to Lightning Girl. Its security was halved and when the Queen—"

"I snatched it right from under your nose!" Mr. Mercury exclaimed and I suddenly saw his large finger waggling before my eyes. "You had no idea I was in the ROOM! I got you again, Aurora, and this time—"

Nolan cleared his throat. Mr. Mercury stopped talking and shuffled backward, away from me.

"*As I was saying,*" Nolan said tiredly, "the crown had less security than normal and Silicon was perfectly placed to take it. When he brought it to me and I held the Jewel of Truth and Nobility in my hand, the first report of dark, overcast skies came in. My new plan came together and now, with the loss of Darek on the inside, I just had to wait patiently for you or Patricia or the Queen to make a mistake and reveal where the other stones were. I'd take them and then you'd come to me. It wasn't long before the mistake was made."

"None of us told a soul," I cried angrily. "We would never put the precious stones in danger."

"You didn't have to tell anyone for me to discover where the other stones were and who was protecting them," he explained calmly. "Selena Silicon told me all that."

"How? How is that possible? I've never met Selena Silicon!"

Nolan cackled. "Yes, you have, dear Lightning Girl! You've met her several times. But her methods of disguise and ability to blend in are even better than those of her brother."

"Well, that's a matter of opinion," Mr. Mercury huffed. "And let's not forget that it was I who—"

"Who is Selena Silicon pretending to be?" I asked impatiently, cutting off grumpy Mr. Mercury. "How have I met her?"

"Why, she's one of Nanny Beam's most trusted agents. Her right-hand woman." Nolan pressed a button on the keyboard and a face came up on all the screens.

I gasped. It was the MI5 agent who had been so nice to me that day at the bowling alley. The agent who had always been at Nanny Beam's side. She was Mr. Mercury's *sister*?

"That's how you knew we were coming to Iceland," Mum said. "She was in the background of Nanny Beam's call to us when we had broken Darek out of prison."

It all suddenly began to make sense. That's why she looked so familiar to me. Now that I thought about it, she had the same sly smile as Mr. Mercury! Mrs. Silicon had even mentioned to us that her daughter had a top secret job. She was a secret agent at MI5, working with Nanny Beam. And she'd been betraying her all this time.

"Selena has been invaluable to my whole operation," Nolan explained triumphantly. "She's been at Nanny Beam's side every step of the way. She managed to tear out that page with the useful information from that precious-stones book while it was in Nanny Beam's custody. Any time that Nanny Beam visited Darek in prison, she brought along her trusted secret service agents. Selena was able to sneak messages from Darek during those visits and send them to me without any suspicion. She kept me updated on every meeting you and Nanny Beam had with the Queen, Aurora."

"Like that was hard?" Mr. Mercury snorted. "I was the one who had to do the actual hard work, but no one cares about—"

"Stop whining, Silicon," Nolan hissed angrily. "Where was I? Oh yes. Aurora, after you begged Nanny Beam and the Queen to check on the other guardians to make sure they were safe, Selena was able to secretly track the locations of the two phone calls Nanny Beam made straight after that meeting. One to the Vatican and one to McLeod Ganj, India. From there, it wasn't too difficult to fill in the gaps."

"The pope and the Dalai Lama are guardians, too?" Aunt Lucinda asked in amazement. "Now our world tour makes much more sense."

"You are the last piece of the puzzle, Aurora. You and the Light of the World," Nolan said. "It's been a long time coming, but it has been worth the wait. Yours is the stone I really want. It's the one that will save me and enhance my powers."

"Enhance?" JJ asked. "You don't have powers. Only the Beam women—"

"Oh, didn't I mention the other charming side effect of the warehouse incident? I'll have to come near the light for this trick and, Silicon, if you wouldn't mind shining your flashlight at the opposite wall."

Mr. Mercury did as he was told. My heart was thudding against my chest at what was about to happen. Nolan approached one of the pools of light, still keeping his face hidden by his hood but pulling his sleeves up so that his arms and hands were on show.

There was a collective gasp as everyone saw what I'd glimpsed earlier. What I had thought looked like his tendons outlined in black marker across his hands was actually every blood vessel of darkness running beneath his skin. Around them, the skin had sunken so that the dark lines protruded boldly. He held his palms toward the wall and I heard him begin to breathe in and out in a slow, controlled pattern.

Suddenly, dark energy beams shot from his palms, hitting the wall lit by Mr. Mercury's flashlight. It was as though he could blast shadows from his hands.

Aunt Lucinda screamed and I heard a sharp intake of breath from Mum behind me as everyone watched in horror.

"The dark energy inside me is expanding," Nolan explained, lowering his hands and letting the sleeves drop to cover his arms again. He steadied himself on the chair next to the books. "I didn't have these powers at first. With the help of the stones, I'll be more powerful than I could have imagined."

"You're mad!" Mum shouted. "The darkness will destroy you! The Light of the World is the source of light, not darkness. How can you think it will help you?"

"Haven't you listened to anything I've said?" he spat back. "I've grown stronger with the precious stones in my presence! They are connected to me now! Enough talk. Aurora." He straightened and began to walk back across the room toward me. "I'm going to need the Light of the World now. I'm guessing it's in one of your pockets. Silicon, if you could do the honors."

I tried backing away as Mr. Mercury loomed toward me, his eyes glinting in the darkness. As I moved, something caught my eye, floating in the pool of light just by the door, which hadn't

been shut properly after the guards had brought us into this room.

It was a feather. An ostrich feather.

I turned my attention back to Mr. Mercury, who was standing just in front of me, ready to start searching my pockets.

"You'll never win against your great nemesis, Mr. Mercury," I declared.

"You're not my great nemesis," he snorted. "My great nemesis is—"

He was cut off by a loud thud as one of the guards standing nearest the door of the tunnel went crashing through the air. Everyone spun round to try and see what was going on as a beam of light appeared, cutting through the darkness. Nolan shrieked, cowering away from the light as it darted about the room.

Mr. Mercury fumbled with his flashlight, managing to turn it on and direct it to the doorway to see the source of the light beam.

An ostrich was standing in the doorway wearing a headlamp.

He spat what looked like a raspberry hard candy across the room, which hit Mr. Mercury in the middle of his forehead with a sharp **THWACK!**

The candy bounced off his head and skittered across the floor.

"Lovely shot, darling!" Aunt Lucinda cried. "And look! It's your nemesis, Mr. Mercury! He was just talking about you."

A wave of hope washed over me.

It was time to fight back.

18

"I HATE THAT OSTRICH!"

Mr. Mercury's cry echoed off the walls as Alfred bolted through the room, making a beeline for his enemy and knocking several of Nolan's guards off balance as he bulldozed his way through.

At Alfred's magnificent entrance, all of us sprang into action.

Several of the men in charge of JJ had either become distracted by the grumpy ostrich lumbering past them at immense speed or been shoved out of the way by him, so none were quite prepared for what JJ did next, which was to bellow a war cry before launching into an incredible swing kick. Owing to his super strength, the one kick sent two of the men next to him flying away toward the walls. Realizing what was going on, another guard jumped on JJ's back, but JJ just grabbed him by the arms and hurled him forward over his head, sending him tumbling to the ground.

"Get the light from him! The light!" Nolan was yelling at Mr. Mercury, as he cowered in the corners of the room, desperately trying to avoid the beam of light from Alfred's headlamp.

As Alfred came pelting toward him, Mr. Mercury looked torn between facing his nemesis head-on or running away from him screaming. He suddenly put up his fists in what I imagine he thought was a threatening stance, but Alfred didn't flinch and he didn't even slow down when he reached his target. He just ran full force at Mr.

Mercury and they collided with a loud **THUD!**

I had closed my eyes at the moment of impact and opened them to find Mr. Mercury on the floor, splayed out like a starfish, while Alfred stood over him, the beam of his headlamp shining on Mr. Mercury's big bald head. With a theatrical flourish, Alfred pinched Mr. Mercury's trousers in his beak and tore them in two to reveal Mr. Mercury's boxer shorts which had sparkly unicorns all over them.

"GERROFF ME, YOU OVERSIZED DUCK!" Mr. Mercury screamed at the top of his lungs.

Alfred froze. Aunt Lucinda gasped dramatically.

"*Oversized duck*? You've really done it now, Mr. Mercury," she tutted.

Steam seemed to be coming out of Alfred's beak. With his large foot square on Mr. Mercury's chest, pinning him to the floor and causing him to flail his arms and legs around in a panic, Alfred slowly lowered his neck so that the end of his beak was touching Mr. Mercury's nose.

"I ... I didn't mean it?" Mr. Mercury attempted in a high-pitched squeak as he stared into the eyes of a VERY cross ostrich.

Alfred ignored him. He pulled his neck back and then launched into such fast pecking on Mr. Mercury's head, the bird's neck and head became a blur.

"Aurora!" Mum yelled. "Get out of here!"

During the commotion, Mum had been busy dealing with the other guards, taking the opportunity of Alfred's entrance to get the upper hand, despite her hands being tied behind her back and locked in the special gloves, so she didn't have any powers.

If I thought my mum was pretty cool before, now I thought she was *awesome*.

I knew that, growing up with Nanny Beam, she probably had some good martial arts skills, and of course being a superhero and everything, I assumed she'd picked up some tips on how to handle herself, but what I did not realize was that she had clearly been inspired or taught by NINJAS.

I've never seen anyone move so fast. I'd barely blinked and she'd whipped the guy behind her right off his feet with a smooth kick to his ankles as she spun round with perfect balance. As another came at her, she sprang into a double roundhouse kick and he fell stumbling backward straight into another guard behind him so they both went down like dominos.

In the meantime, the guard in charge of Aunt Lucinda was yowling in pain and hopping on one leg after she'd stomped on his foot as hard as possible with her stiletto heel.

"That will teach you to be a bad guy!" Aunt Lucinda huffed, sticking her nose in the air.

"Aurora! Go!" Mum called out again.

I made a run for it, darting toward the door that was now fully open, thanks to Alfred's entrance, but I felt a strong grip on my arm and I was pulled backward.

"Not so fast, Lightning Girl!" Darek growled. "Give me the stone!"

A blur came rushing past me and rugby-tackled Darek to the ground, leaving me free to go. I glanced back to see Darek winded and writhing on the floor, while JJ stood over him, giving me a thumbs-up.

"Go, Lightning Girl! Get that stone to safety. We'll handle everything here!"

My hands still tied behind my back, I dodged the chaos surrounding me and slid through the door back into the underground tunnel. Running through the dark was much harder than walking through it and this time I didn't have anyone with a flashlight in front of me or Darek holding me up as I went. I hurtled forward blindly, hoping that the tunnel was shorter than I thought.

I collided with the wall painfully, knocking me to my knees, remembering too late that the tunnel had curved to the left on the way down. On the ground, I heard footsteps and the heavy breathing of someone running after me.

"Come back here, Aurora Beam!"

The threatening voice echoed down the tunnel and my heart leapt into my mouth as I realized it was Nolan. He must have slipped out without the others noticing.

I had to get to the entrance of the tunnel, out into the light. With all the energy I could muster, I pulled myself to my feet using the wall to leverage me up and then raced on as quickly as possible, tripping over my feet, my arm grazing one side of the wall as I used it for guidance.

Nolan was getting closer, his eyes so used to the dark that the pitch-black of the tunnel didn't matter to him. My heart was thudding hard against my chest and the adrenaline was making my ears ring.

I saw the entrance to the tunnel up ahead and desperately ran toward it. Suddenly, something went swooshing past my ear, like a strong gust of wind. A moment later, it happened again, swishing past me and nearly sending me off balance.

I felt sick as I realized it was Nolan shooting

his dark energy beams from his palms at me. I didn't have much room to dodge them in the tunnel and if hit, they were definitely strong enough to knock me to the ground. The only good thing was that Nolan slowed a little, as shooting each dark beam wiped his energy.

All I could do was aim for that opening and run faster than I've ever run before.

Ducking as a ball of darkness shot over my head and cracked against the rocks above me, I

pushed through the entrance to the tunnel and stumbled outside.

Any hope I'd had for daylight putting off Nolan from emerging after me fizzled away. It was dark outside, the skies murky and shadowed. The aurora borealis flickered dimly, fading away with every minute.

My shock at the sky cost me. Pausing to look up, I was sent flying forward by a blow of dark energy that grazed my left side. Without my hands to stop my fall, I was lucky that the force toppled me slightly sideways so that my left arm took most of the impact, rather than me landing flat on my face.

Nolan cackled triumphantly as he approached, out of breath from the chase. I tried wriggling along the ground, but he laughed maniacally at my attempt, catching up with me easily and pinning me to the ground with his foot.

"It's over, Lightning Girl. It's finally over."

Standing over me, Nolan slowly lifted his hood and revealed his face which, like his arms and hands, was horrifically scarred with lines of darkness that looked etched into his skin.

I'd been expecting that.

What I hadn't been expecting was Nanny Beam's eyes and nose. I'd seen an old photograph of Nolan, so I knew they looked alike, but for some reason his horrible, evil plans and actions had led me to think that any Beam characteristics would have been long gone, even the physical ones. That his face was so familiar made everything he was doing feel even more painful.

"Look where we are," he continued, towering over me and oblivious to my scrutinizing his features as I blinked up at him. "Right underneath the aurora borealis."

He pointed up at the sky. He grinned, showing crooked yellow teeth.

"I have the guardian and you have the Light of the World, which means that I can transfer the powers." He shook his head at me pityingly. "You should have stayed indoors, Aurora. Yet again, you've run straight into a situation that works best for me and now you're stuck in the middle of nowhere with no one to help you. Tell me, what are the Beam women without their light-beam powers?"

"What do you mean?" I croaked, my brain running through ideas and not coming up with anything. All I could think to do was keep him talking and bide my time.

"The answer to my question is: nothing. You're *nothing* without your powers."

"That's what you think of Patricia, right? Nanny Beam," I said, his face wincing at her name. "Everyone admired her powers but, other than that, she was nothing special in your eyes."

"Precisely," he said, lifting his hands up to examine his palms. "I was a prodigy. I built an empire. I moved technology forward at a faster pace than anyone else. I achieved more than anyone could imagine and yet next to her, I was ignored by our parents. Still, after today, that will all be in the past. We had better start; the darkness is growing. I need the power of all four of the precious stones."

He showed me his palms and I saw another faint black line appear, swirling beneath his skin, growing darker and bolder. He then reached into my coat pocket and I wriggled under his grip, but it was no use. He pulled out the box and gave me a thin-lipped smile.

"I trust Nanny Beam had this box specially made for the Light of the World," he said.

"You won't be able to get in. Only my mum knows the codes."

He looked down at me, tilting his head to one side. "You have so much to learn, Aurora. I've already told you that when it comes to superheroes, they're exceptionally predictable."

He tapped the side of the box and a keypad appeared, along with a series of small blinking lights across the top of the box. He delicately entered some codes and, one by one, each light turned green.

"And the final hurdle," he said, examining the bottom of the box, which had a tiny red light embedded into it that I hadn't noticed.

I was staring at him in disbelief, too shocked at how easily he'd gotten past the security measures to realize what he was doing as he suddenly held the bright light close to my face.

Lifting it away, it was now blinking green.

"Eye retina scanner," he explained. "Only for Beam women. Really, Patricia, couldn't you have been more imaginative?"

The box clicked open. He gently lifted the lid and his eyes lit up as he saw the stone. Being so close to the source of my powers sent a strange rush of warmth from my toes all the way up my body and down my arms, making my fingers tingle. Near the Light of the World, my powers were almost uncontrollable and my gloves began to shake from the light energy building up in my hands.

"How do you think you are going to transfer the powers?" I asked. "You have to take off my gloves for that and as soon as you do, I'm just going to summon my powers and—"

"One moment of pain for a lifetime of power," he said, lifting the stone from the box and clasping his fingers round it. "It will be worth it. Years of hiding away in the darkness and now it is finally time."

As he clutched the Light of the World, I looked beyond him up at the sky and saw that the aurora borealis seemed . . . a little brighter?

I squinted at it to work out whether I was seeing things. Maybe the fall to the ground had made my vision a bit hazy? No, I could see clearly and the northern lights were *definitely* brighter.

It didn't make any sense. And yet. . .

My powers were bubbling up inside without me having to concentrate on summoning them. I should have been feeling terrible, distraught at what was about to happen, but I didn't feel bad.

I felt *brilliant*. I could feel the sparks shooting from my fingertips and the swirled scar on my left palm burning within the gloves. Light within me was trying to find a way of shining out.

I looked back at Nolan with the stone in his hands, and I couldn't help but smile.

He opened his mouth to say something, but then he saw my expression and his face fell.

"What? Why are you smiling?" he asked, his eyes darting about, worried that someone was coming to help. "I shut and locked that door to the tunnel behind me as I came after you; no one is coming to your rescue."

"I know," I replied calmly. "I don't need anyone to rescue me."

His brow furrowed in confusion. "What's going on? Are you ... *glowing*?"

"Don't you know how powerful the Beam

women really are, especially when we're around the source of all our powers?" I asked breezily from the ground. "Did you really think that a pair of gloves designed by some *guy* in an underground lair was going to stop us?"

His expression turned to panic as he looked at the precious stone resting in his palm. When he'd picked it up earlier, he'd dropped the box to the ground and he quickly went to retrieve it. But he was too late.

A surge came rushing through me with a force more powerful than it had ever been before. Warm and tingling, the energy shot down my arms, my fingers growing even more fiery than they already were, and suddenly. . .

WHOOOOOOSH!

The gloves disintegrated into nothing as light beams exploded from my palms like immense lightning bolts. It was my powers but like they'd never been before: a force of dazzling, pure bright light bursting out of my hands. It was so powerful it knocked Nolan clean off me and onto his back. He cried in pain and covered his face as waves of glittering light flooded across the land surrounding us.

The Light of the World fell to the ground, rolling across the grass.

As the energy force slowly waned and my hands were still sparking, I stood up and picked up the stone with my left hand, letting its pattern sit on my matching swirled scar.

Nolan scrambled to his feet, turning to look at me, his eyes wide with fear, and then his expression clouded over with anger. He began to determinedly shoot out dark energy bolts from his hands.

I quickly dodged them and, careful not to drop the precious stone, held up my hands to let the powers rush down my arm without any effort. The beams blasted from my palms, the pure

radiant light hitting the dark energy head on.

Nolan's dark powers were no match for the Light of the World.

The light engulfed the darkness and he dropped to the floor, crying out as he was bathed in the glowing beams.

There was suddenly a roaring sound from the sky as secret service helicopters appeared, hovering above us.

"Finally. Well done, Cherry!" I grinned, waving up at them before turning to Nolan, who was cowering on the ground and had shielded himself from the helicopter spotlights with his hood. "I think it's about time you saw your sister again. Don't you?"

20

"This is it. This is the place."

Standing at the top of Mount Kirkjufell, everything seemed so small. After a two-hour trek to get there, the view was incredible and I could see for miles. There was no question that this was where I was supposed to be. As Mum and I had followed our guide up the winding mountain path to the top, the swirled scar on my hand had begun to glow.

The guide, who was from the local town of Grundarfjörður (and had laughed at me for a

full five minutes as I tried to pronounce that),
pointed up to the sky.

"There you have it. The aurora borealis," he
said, beaming at me. "This is the best view you
can get, in my opinion."

"It's beautiful," Mum agreed.

He hesitated and then held up his phone
apologetically. "I'm sorry to ask this, but could
I have a photo with you, Lightning Girl? I'm a
big fan."

"Of course!"

Mum took a few photos of us and then
handed him back his phone. He scrolled
excitedly through the many pictures.

"Thank you so much," he gushed, before
nodding back to the path. "I'll give you a
moment to enjoy the northern lights. I'll be
over there."

We thanked him and then waited until he
was out of earshot as he headed back down the

path and out of sight, busy sending the photo to all his friends.

Mum inhaled deeply. "I can't believe we're finally here."

"I know. Everything has been such a whirlwind. At least it's over now."

Mum nodded. I was glad Mum had stayed on with me after everyone else had returned to England, so that I didn't have to do this alone. We were still digesting what had happened, especially the revelation that Nolan Vermore had been alive all this time.

When Nanny Beam came parachuting down from one of the secret service helicopters yesterday – I spotted her among the other agents floating down from the sky, as she had a personal parachute which was the Union Jack flag with a lightning bolt across it – she'd landed and then stood frozen to the spot, staring at Nolan as her agents pounced on him

and tore his hood back, revealing his disfigured but recognizable face.

She'd looked as though she'd seen a ghost. Which, I guess, she kind of had.

She hadn't made a sound, but I saw her mouth the word "Nolan" as she watched him being pulled to his feet, a tear running down her cheek.

"Nanny Beam!" I cried out at the top of my lungs, pointing at the agent standing just behind her. "She's Selena Silicon! She's been betraying you all this time!"

Horrified, Nanny Beam turned around to face her. Selena started to back away slowly, her eyes darting around nervously at all the MI5 agents staring at her in shock.

"It's lies," she said hurriedly, shaking her head. "It's all lies!"

"She's been feeding Nolan information about the precious stones," I shouted. "She warned him that we were coming here to Iceland so he could set a trap. She's Mr. Mercury's sister!"

"*No*," Nanny Beam said, as Selena continued to retreat toward the helicopter.

Suddenly, Selena's expression transitioned from innocent and frightened to sly and determined. She spun round quick as a flash and darted toward the helicopter. The other agents raced after her, but there was no need.

Nanny Beam lifted her hands and cried, "**SHABEAM!**" Light beams blasted from her palms with such force that Selena Silicon was knocked to the floor, as though struck by a lightning bolt. Two more agents grabbed her while she was lying dazed on the ground, pulling her to her feet.

"Don't let her out of your sight," Nanny Beam instructed her agents, her voice filled with disgust.

She then turned back to see Nolan being escorted toward her.

"Get him back to London, too. I'll deal with both of them there."

Before anyone came to fuss over me, I hurriedly put the Light of the World back in its box and safely tucked it into my pocket. I told the agents that came to check that I was fine, but they insisted on doing all these tests to make sure. After I told them about the tunnel, they went to save the others from the underground lair, while I went over to Nanny Beam. I had never seen her look so vulnerable.

She wrapped her arms around me. I couldn't think of what to say so we stood in silence for a while, and then I spoke.

"Nice touch yelling '**SHABEAM**' just then."

She laughed through her tears. "I thought it added a bit of flair."

We stood there hugging until Mum emerged from the tunnel and ran over, relieved to see that I was OK and Nolan's plan had been foiled.

"I knew you wouldn't let him win," she said, tears running down her face as she held me so tightly I could barely breathe. "I knew it."

Then, she turned to Nanny Beam and, with Aunt Lucinda who came tottering over to us, still in her heels, we had a big Beam group hug.

"My girls," Nanny Beam whispered, before drawing back and giving us a weak smile. "I have a lot to sort out back in London. Can I leave everything that's still to do here to you, Aurora?"

I patted the precious stone box in my pocket. "I've got it covered."

Mum put a hand on Nanny Beam's arm. "Mum, we should talk about Nolan and how—"

"Another time, Kiyana," Nanny Beam said gently. "I'll be all right."

With that, she gave us a sharp nod and then switched into MI5 mode, wiping her tears away and barking orders at her agents, before marching toward one of the helicopters waiting for her. She climbed into the front seat next to the pilot and put on a headset, and the helicopter flew off into the distance.

I felt sick with worry about her, but I didn't have too much time to dwell on it as Cherry came running over to check that I was OK, and then JJ and Alfred came to stand with us because the pope and the Dalai Lama wanted to thank us all for rescuing them.

It was quite a surreal moment, if I'm honest.

We then all watched Mr. Mercury, Darek and all their guards being led away in handcuffs by the secret service agents. Mr. Mercury and Darek were still bickering and busy blaming the other one for everything as they were led up into a helicopter.

Mr. Mercury spotted Selena being held next to the helicopter he was about to be led into and he rolled his eyes and said, "Here I was thinking my day couldn't get any worse! PLEASE tell me I don't have to sit next to *you*."

He looked at one of the agents escorting him and said in a pleading voice, "Any chance I can go back to London in a different helicopter than *her*?"

"Like any of this is MY fault?" Selena yelled at him thunderously. "Everything on my end went perfectly to plan. But then Lightning Girl gets here and you lot mess it all up!"

"Yeah? Well YOU try wrestling a gigantic ostrich! I'd like to see you try to win that battle."

She snorted. "Oh please, I could win against an ostrich any day. You're completely useless at everything. Just like Mummy says."

Mr. Mercury flinched as though someone had slapped him across the face. "HOW DARE YOU BRING MUMMY INTO THIS?"

"Touched a nerve have I, Desmond?" Selena replied smugly. "You wait until Mummy hears about what you've done now. Stealing the Imperial State Crown from the Queen; kidnapping Lightning Girl. She's going to be FURIOUS! You'll be grounded until the next century!"

"What about you?" he seethed, his face red as a tomato. "She's always been so proud of her darling daughter, the top secret spy. HA! She won't be so proud when she hears about your part in all this."

"Yeah, well YOU—"

"All right, enough of this," one of the agents interrupted in a tired voice. "All of you are coming in this helicopter. No arguments."

"No, please!" Mr. Mercury cried. "Don't make me sit with her! It's torture! Her voice is so GRATING! I had to put up with it my whole childhood!"

"Please don't make me sit in there with him!" Selena begged. "He's so annoying! Plus, he smells. Can't I go in that helicopter over there?"

"If anyone is going in a different helicopter, it should be ME!" Darek argued. "PLEASE do not put me in the same one as these two bickering idiots!"

"You should have all thought about this before you decided to team up together and try to take over the world with your evil plans," the secret service agent barked impatiently. "Now, in you get!"

Stifling our giggles, we watched as they were escorted into the helicopter one by one, Selena Silicon managing to kick Mr. Mercury's ankle as he went up the steps, causing him to fall flat on his face, much to her pleasure. Once he was back on his feet with the help of an MI5 agent, he tried to get his revenge by kicking back at her. But he missed and kicked Darek's shin instead. Darek howled in pain.

As the door shut behind them, the last thing we heard was Darek swearing his vengeance on

Mr. Mercury.

"Good riddance," Mum sighed, leaning her head on Aunt Lucinda's shoulder.

After we'd been checked over again by the agents to make sure we really were OK, like we were insisting, we were offered a lift back home. Cherry and JJ happily hopped into one of the helicopters, along with the pope and the Dalai Lama, desperate to ask the MI5 agents a million questions about their job, none of which they were allowed to answer.

Aunt Lucinda offered to wait around with Alfred for a couple of days while we finished our mission and then fly us home in her car. We found a hotel in the nearby town, had the best night's sleep we'd had in a long time and woke up, ready for the big day ahead. Over breakfast, Aunt Lucinda let out a long sigh.

"Four precious stones with powers..." She smiled mischievously. "Priceless jewels and gems. Think how good they'd look on me!"

"I'm glad we have the answers to everything now," Mum said, ignoring her. "It all makes sense."

"Almost everything. I still don't understand who visited Darek in prison," I pointed out, still troubled by this tiny factor. "I saw their visit in the logbook, but it can't have been Nolan. He really couldn't go into the light."

"It must have been Mr. Mercury – or should I say Mr. Silicon – in disguise. Or Selena Silicon maybe."

"I don't think any of them will be getting any prison visitors this time round," Aunt Lucinda said. "I hope they've learned their lessons. I suppose if Mr. Mercury ever needs reminding, Alfred would be happy to pop in and see him."

She then stood up and announced that she was heading off for the day. She and Alfred were going to the Blue Lagoon Spa.

"One of the twenty-five wonders of the world," Aunt Lucinda declared, sliding into the driver's seat as Alfred sat in the back of the car, ready to go. "Ostriches are particularly partial to geothermal seawater. And the Icelandic cuisine at the restaurant is to die for. But enjoy your . . . sweaty hike! Toodle-loo!"

But no matter what Aunt Lucinda thought, there really was nowhere I'd rather be than standing under the northern lights after walking up this mountain.

Up here, looking out at the view, I felt so calm and peaceful.

I hadn't really felt that in months.

"So, what do you think we're looking for?" Mum asked, putting her hands on her hips, her eyes scanning the rock beneath our feet.

"I think we'll know when we see it," I said hopefully.

We both began to walk slowly about,

examining the ground as carefully as possible. Then, I saw it. An indent in the rock at the highest point of the mountain. So small, no one would notice it. But it was the delicate, swirled pattern in the indent that caught my eye.

"Here," I called to Mum, who came rushing over to stand next to me.

"You've found it. You've really found it," Mum whispered, her eyes filling with tears. "The exact place where the Light of the World was first found, centuries ago, under the aurora borealis."

I pulled the box out from my pocket and opened it, revealing the precious stone sitting in the middle. My palms immediately began to glow and so did Mum's, sparks flying from our fingers.

"You should do this on your own. But I'll be right behind you," Mum said calmly, kissing my head and then stepping back to stand a few feet away.

I took a deep breath and lifted the Light of the World from the box. I knelt and held the precious stone in my hand, gently tracing the swirl on it with my finger.

"It's time," I said to no one but myself.

I set the stone into the mountain. A wave of dazzling light rushed through me the moment I placed it down.

"Aurora! Look!" Mum gasped, holding out her hand to help me to my feet and gazing up at the sky.

Magical glowing lights of every color stretched across the sky as the aurora borealis shone like never before.

THE DAI

LIGHT T

OVE

SCIEN

DISAPPEARIN

Special report by Henry Nib

Meteorologists have been left stumped by the strange phenomenon across the skies that saw a random darkness which now seems to have entirely disappeared.

Reports began in December of a noticeably darker atmosphere, affecting several regions the United Kingdom as well as many countri across the world, but after months of specu

Y SCOPE

IUMPHS
DARK

S BAFFLED BY
ARKNESS PHENOMENON

xtensive research as to the cause of the
, the darkness has now vanished, and the
s have seemingly returned to normal.
I simply can't explain it," said Gilbert Granite,
a science professor. "The darkness was worrying,
causing widespread panic, and now it has gone
without any known source."

A team of Northern Lights enthusiasts is also
currently trying to explain why the aurora is
brighter than ever before, with many surmising
that there may be a connection between the two.

"It's truly miraculous," meteorology professor
Bella Breeze said. "It seemed that darkness was
descending on our planet, but light saved the day.
Literally!"

THE WEEK

OSTRICH H
BY POF
RECOVERII
PRICELESS

Special report by Olive Folio

The pope has bestowed a medal upon an ostrich, after the bird discovered a priceless canvas which had bee stolen from the Vatican earlier this month. Returning th *Madonna of Foligno* by Renaissance painter Raphael to rightful place, the ostrich was hailed by the pope for hi kind and selfless actions, before being rewarded the to honor that can be bestowed upon an animal.

HERALD

NORED
FOR
MISSING
AINTING!

A statue of the ostrich, which will be erected in St. Peter's Square, has also been commissioned. Her Majesty the Queen commented that he was "a true hero and inspiration to us all" when she heard the news.

The ostrich, who has not been named and is unavailable for comment due to his admirable modesty, was last seen at auditions for the forthcoming opera at Rome's famous Teatro dell'Opera.

21

"Here we are," Nanny Beam said, getting out of the car ahead of me and clutching the box to her. "Welcome to the Royal stables."

I followed her in and someone came out from behind one of the horses, wearing a patched-up, mucky coat and holding a grooming mitt and a thick-bristled brush. At first I thought it was someone who worked there, but I quickly curtsied as I realized it was the Queen.

"Good morning, Patricia." She smiled warmly, as the horse began nibbling at her shoulder. "And good morning, Aurora. It's lovely to see you both. Excuse my appearance, I was just giving Lord Barnaby here a groom." She put the brush and mitt down and stroked the horse's nose affectionately. "Magnificent, isn't he?"

"He really is," I agreed, stepping forward and reaching up so that I could give his mane a pat. "And Lord Barnaby is a great name."

"Thank you," she said, and chuckled. "I love sneaking out to the stables whenever I can. I never feel calmer than when I'm around animals. It sounds odd, but one might even say they seem to ... understand me a little better than people do."

I nodded. "I get that. I feel the same about my dog, Kimmy."

"I remember her from the medal ceremony," the Queen said, reaching into her pocket to hold out some oats for Lord Barnaby to gobble up eagerly from her palm. "She looked very elegant in her big red bow."

Her eyes drifted to the box that Nanny Beam was holding and she inhaled sharply, blinking back tears. "Is that. . ."

Nanny Beam stepped forward and held it out to give to her. I took it and then, looking round me to make sure that the stables were empty except for us, opened the box and revealed the Imperial State Crown.

The sapphire at the very top glinted in the light. The Queen brushed the rest of the oats from her hands – much to Lord Barnaby's delight, who promptly hoovered them up from the floor – and took the box carefully.

"You did it," the Queen whispered. "*You really did it.*"

"The Jewel of Truth and Nobility is back where it belongs," I said firmly. "Just like the other precious stones."

She lifted her eyes to meet mine, shutting the lid of the box. "Thank you, Lightning Girl."

"You're welcome, Your Majesty," I said, giggling as Lord Barnaby began sniffing at my cheek, which really tickled. "And if it ever goes missing again, you know where I am."

Nanny Beam laughed, coming over to put an arm round me and give Lord Barnaby a pat on the neck.

"You know, Aurora, I think after this adventure, you deserve a bit of a break from saving the world," the Queen said. "Don't you?"

*

"I'm so happy you're back, Aurora," Kizzy said, rolling her sleeves up to get her arms in the sun. "Are you sure you're feeling completely better? Your flu must have been really bad."

"I'm fine, promise," I assured her. "I missed you all so much."

It was a lovely sunny day and we were sitting on one of the benches outside during our lunch break. With only a week to go before Easter vacation, everyone was starting to get in vacation mode. Everyone except for me, that is. Due to the number of days I'd missed, I had a pile of homework the size of the Eiffel Tower.

("Don't worry," Kizzy had told me excitedly on my first day back. "I made sure to note down every piece of homework we were given while you were sick, so you wouldn't miss out on ANYTHING." Why was I friends with her again?)

"School wasn't the same without you," Suzie said, taking a sip of apple juice. "There was no one to yell at during gym class for being so slow. It wasn't right."

Kizzy and I shared a smile, and Georgie burst out laughing.

"Thanks, Suzie. I think." I giggled. "I'm sorry I missed you winning another gymnastics competition. Someone filmed your routine, though, right? Why don't you all come over to mine tonight for a viewing?"

Fred groaned dramatically, slumping his head forward into his hands.

"We have to sit through it AGAIN?" he complained.

"Nice try, Fred, but you're not fooling

us," Georgie said, prodding his arm. "You were spellbound during Suzie's routine at the competition. How did you describe it again?"

"I don't remember," he sniffed.

"I do!" Kizzy smiled. "You described it as 'unbelievable.'"

"You hear that, Aurora?" Suzie grinned triumphantly. "Even my worst critics thought it *unbelievable*."

"Whatever." Fred frowned. "I'll only come over tonight if I can pick the pizza toppings."

"Deal." I held out my hand to shake Fred's.

"What's it like without Alfred and Aunt Lucinda living with you?" Kizzy asked. "It must be quite nice having your space back."

"I guess so."

Kizzy was half right. It was nice not to be so crowded, but with Cherry and JJ having gone home too, the house felt weirdly empty. When we got back from Iceland, Mum filled the family in on what they needed to know, while I got pinned to the floor by Kimmy, who tried to slobber me to death. Dad had cooked an amazing meal and we'd sat round the table together, laughing and joking about Clara's idea of distracting the agents and how Alexis hacked into a high-security prison system.

"Nanny Beam gave me the biggest lecture about that," Alexis had told us, rolling his eyes. "I never thought I'd hear the end of it."

"She did offer you a job with the MI5 tech team for the future, though," Dad had pointed out. "So, that's something."

"Yeah." Alexis had grinned. "That's something."

"And while you were away in Iceland, an envelope came for Clara with some exciting news," Dad had said, winking at her.

"I got into the most prestigious science

summer camp in the country," she said matter-of-factly, helping herself to some potatoes. "It's meant to be for age thirteen upward, but they've decided to make an exception for me, which is very nice."

Mum and I had screamed and smothered her with a congratulatory hug, causing Kimmy to bark loudly in excitement and chase her tail madly, no idea why we were so happy but wanting to join in anyway.

I was glad so much was going on at home to keep me distracted, but my room felt too big without Cherry's mattress in it too, and I missed Aunt Lucinda's constant cheerfulness and sense of fun.

I even missed Alfred a little bit. Which weird, considering he'd torn up so many of my clothes that he'd found in my hiding place under the bed and stolen my Lightning Girl sunglasses.

Luckily, Georgie designed me a new pair to cheer me up after being sick for so long.

I pushed them up my nose now as Suzie held out her phone to show us a picture online of Mr. Mercury and Selena Silicon being escorted by police from a van toward a prison.

"It's all over the news," she said. "The crown has been returned to the Queen. I hope Mr. Mercury never gets out of prison again. I can't believe that his sister was in on it, too! I wonder how Nanny Beam caught them both."

"I can't help but feel sorry for Mrs. Silicon," Georgie said. "She was so nice and she must be so upset with both her children."

"Nanny Beam actually filled me in on that side of things," I revealed with a smile. "Mrs. Silicon is furious. She told Nanny Beam that she's going to visit them in prison every day and for the whole visitor's hour, for each of them, she's going to practice her recorder right in their ears."

The Bright Sparks all grimaced.

"I can't say they don't deserve it," Kizzy said.

"Mrs. Silicon also told Nanny Beam that we were delightful," I added. "Georgie, she said if you ever need help with any alterations or sewing for your future fashion shows, she'd like to be considered."

"Noted," Georgie said. "The summer fashion show I'm organizing is just around the corner. I'm going to need all the help I can get over vacation."

"Mr. Mercury is in prison, the crown is back with the Queen and, most importantly..." Kizzy lowered her voice, glancing round to make sure no other students were listening. "The Light of the World has been returned to its rightful place. It's all worked out in the end and MI5 didn't even need our help."

I smiled to myself as the others nodded in agreement.

Fred sighed. "I have to admit that when you

told us Nanny Beam had returned the stone, Aurora, I felt a little disappointed."

"You did?"

"Yeah. It's great and everything, but I wish I could have been there to see it, you know?"

"I know what you mean," Suzie said, getting a dreamy look on her face. "Imagine being under the northern lights and watching the most precious stone in the world be returned to its rightful place. It's like a scene from a movie. It must have been amazing."

"Yeah." Kizzy smiled at me sympathetically. "I'm sorry you were too sick to go with her to return it, Aurora. That must have been terrible."

"It's OK," I said hurriedly. "I'm just happy to be back at school with the Bright Sparks. Everything is back to normal and we don't have anything to worry about except homework."

"True." Suzie smiled, closing her eyes and lifting her face to the sun. "As Nanny Beam always says, we should enjoy the peace, calm and positive energy of these sun rays. Let our souls blossom and regenerate our light within."

We all sat in thoughtful silence, Suzie's lovely words hanging in the air.

The silence lasted for precisely five seconds before Fred reached for something in his bag and then jumped to his feet, holding a super-soaker water gun.

"SURPRISE ATTACK!" he yelled, aiming it straight at Suzie and drenching her.

Suzie screamed, attracting the

attention of everyone outside, who all looked over to see what was going on.

"I'M GOING TO KILL YOU!" Suzie raged, her wet hair plastered to her face, as Fred roared with laughter.

He stopped laughing though when she ran full pelt at him, managing to wrestle the super soaker from his hands and chasing him round, getting him back. Students began to cheer as the two of them ran round and round in circles and I even saw Mrs. Prime, the headmistress, stifling some giggles before she called out for them both to "stop messing around."

"What was that Suzie was saying about peace and calm?" Kizzy asked, shaking her head at them.

"So, Aurora, what are you going to do without a mission to focus on?" Georgie asked, sniggering as Suzie got Fred right in the face just as he was turning around to ask her to let him catch his breath. "Now that Mr. Mercury has finally been tracked down and, as you say, everything is back to normal, don't you think you'll get bored?"

"Nah." I grinned. "I'm all right. Knowing Lightning Girl and the Bright Sparks, another adventure will find us soon enough. Until then, I'm happy to just be me."

I closed my eyes, feeling the warmth of the sunshine on my face, listening to Georgie and Kizzy burst into a fresh round of laughter as Fred frantically raced past, Suzie hot on his heels.

Everything was just as it should be.

EPILOGUE

In the darkness, Nolan Vermore lay on the rock-hard mattress and stared up at the gray ceiling. He closed his eyes and exhaled deeply, wondering how everything could have gone so wrong.

He had been so close to ultimate power. So close to having everything he dreamed of in his grasp. And then that Beam girl had ruined everything. A member of his own family, no less.

Now, he was stuck here. In a tiny cell in the most secure prison in the world. He was so bored. There was nothing to do, the food was disgusting, and he'd hardly been able to sleep a wink, the room smelled so damp and his bed was too uncomfortable.

And considering he'd lived in a cave for decades, that was really saying something.

At least they'd put him in an empty underground cell, so that he could be in the pitch black. He supposed that was considered a punishment in most people's eyes, but Nolan still couldn't bear the light.

He lifted his hand right up to his face and opened his eyes to examine his palm. He could make out more of the thin, dark, jagged lines protruding from his sunken skin.

His door suddenly opened, and someone stepped in, closing the door firmly behind them.

Nolan sat up and squinted through the darkness.

"Who are you?" he barked. "Who's there?"

"Hello, Nolan," came the reply.

"What's going on?"

"I'm here to talk to you. I have a feeling that we can help each other."

"What?" Nolan frowned. "Who are you?"

"You see," the voice continued, "I visited your son, Darek, when he was in prison. He gave me some *very* useful information. I think that I may be able to help you and, in return, *you* may be able to help *me*."

Nolan slowly got up from his bed and peered into the gloom. This stranger's voice gave him a very uncomfortable feeling and it took Nolan a few moments to work out exactly what that alien feeling was: fear. He hadn't felt afraid of anyone in a very long time. Usually, everyone was afraid of him.

Not this visitor, though.

"Who are you?" Nolan demanded once

more, too nervous to approach them.

The stranger stepped forward and as they got closer, Nolan saw their face. He gasped.

"*You*," he whispered.

"Yes, Nolan," the visitor replied, a thin smile appearing on their lips. "It's me."

ACKNOWLEDGEMENTS

I can't believe we are on book 4! The journey has been amazing! I have so many people to thank for making this dream possible. It takes a fabulous team of driven, focused, creative people to make something a success and I feel like the luckiest girl to have the most exceptional team of people around me that are a joy to work with! :) Lauren Fortune, Aimee Stewart, Mary Jones, Kate Graham, Eishar Brar and the whole team at Scholastic; Katy Birchall, Lauren Gardner, Steve Simpson, James Lancett and Rob Parkinson.

Thank you from the bottom of my heart! Lightning Girl
has been one of the most fun projects I have worked on
in a long time and it's down to all of you for making
it so special. We set out to inspire young readers but I
too have been inspired and motivated to keep creating
fabulous stories that make a real difference.

A big thank you to the A Team, friends and family for
your continued love and support. And thank you once
again to all the readers who make it all worthwhile!

Love and light,

ALESHA X

Photo by John Wright

ALESHA DIXON first found fame as part of Brit-nominated and Mobo Award-winning group Mis-teeq, which achieved 2 platinum albums and 7 top ten hits, before going on to become a platinum-selling solo artist in her own right. Alesha's appearance on *Strictly Come Dancing* in 2007 led to her winning the series and becoming a judge for three seasons.

Since then she has presented and hosted many UK TV shows including CBBC dance show *Alesha's Street Dance Stars, Children In Need, Sport Relief, Your Face Sounds Familiar* and ITV's *Dance, Dance, Dance*. She is a hugely popular judge on *Britain's Got Talent*.

"My inspiration to create a superhero called Lightning Girl began with wanting my young daughter to feel empowered. It's been a dream to create a strong role model that any child can look up to - I want my readers to see themselves in Aurora, who is dealing with trouble at home and trouble at school alongside her new powers.

I also have a love of precious stones and their healing properties; I have always been fascinated with their spectacular colors and the positive energy that they bring. As human beings we are always searching for something greater within ourselves and a deeper meaning to life and it's my belief that we all have a light within us that can affect change and bring good to the world... we just have to harness it! :)

Enter **AURORA BEAM!**"

Photo by Ian Arnold

Katy Birchall is the author of the side-splittingly funny *The It Girl: Superstar Geek*, *The It Girl: Team Awkward*, *The It Girl: Don't Tell the Bridesmaid* and the *Hotel Royale* series, *Secrets of a Teenage Heiress* and *Dramas of a Teenage Heiress*. Katy also works as a freelance journalist and has written a non-fiction book, *How to be a Princess: Real-Life Fairy Tales for Modern Heroines*.

Katy won the 24/7 Theatre Festival Award for Most Promising New Comedy Writer with her very serious play about a ninja monkey at a dinner party.

When she isn't busy writing, she is reading biopics of Jane Austen, daydreaming about being an elf in *The Lord of the Rings*, or running across a park chasing her rescue dog, Bono, as he chases his arch nemesis: squirrels.

THE BRIGHT SPARKS

Aurora Beam:
Lightning Girl

Fred Pepe: President
of the Bright Sparks

Cherry Mirella

Benjamin Jackson Jr.
("JJ")

Georgie Taylor:
Stylist

Kizzy Carpenter:
The Brains

Kimmy

Suzie Bravo/Flexi-Girl

WHICH BRIGHT SPARK ARE YOU?

Think you've got what it takes to be one of Aurora Beam's best friends,

THE BRIGHT SPARKS?

Take this quiz to find out who you're most like ...

What's your favorite thing to do on a Saturday?

A Playing an elaborate practical joke on your pals, ideally involving some ants in their pants.

B Hanging out at a cool café, people watching and secretly listening in on conversations.

C Playing in a soccer tournament – you're very competitive.

D Going clothes shopping to pick the perfect outfit.

E Spending the entire day in the library – bliss.

F Practicing your gymnastic routine until it's perfect.

G Eating cookies!

At a school friend's party, what are you most likely to be doing?

A Hiding behind a door ready to jump out at someone and give them a fright.

B Plugging in your headphones to listen to your favorite music – you're a bit cool for all this childish chat.

C Showing off trying to impress everyone by lifting up the kitchen table one-handed.

D Raiding your host's closet upstairs to see if they've got any fabulous accessories you can borrow.

E Sitting quietly behind the sofa with a really good book.

F Trying to organize a dance-off, secretly convinced you'll be the winner.

G Sniffing everyone's pockets trying to find cookies!

What's your favorite animal?

A A fun-loving hyena

B A cool and collected cat

C A brave and loud lion

D A perfectly styled peacock

E A quiet and clever owl

F An athletic and graceful gazelle

G A dog, obviously

What would your superhero motto be?

A Beware the Joker in the Pack

B Looking to the Future

C I Break Down Walls for Breakfast

D Saving the Day in Style

E The Pen is Mightier than the Sword

F I'm a Top of the Leaderboard Type

G Will Be Courageous For Cookies

ANSWERS

MOSTLY A – you're Fred Pepe, the clown of the group – always in trouble but with a heart of gold!

MOSTLY B – you're cool, calm and collected Cherry Mirella, the girl with the supersonic hearing and ability to see the future!

MOSTLY C – you're the self-crowned king of the pack, JJ Jackson – strong, loyal and brave!

MOSTLY D – you're the ever-stylish, uber-creative Georgie Taylor – always dressed to impress!

MOSTLY E – you're Kizzy Carpenter, Aurora's best friend and the sweetest, smartest, kindest girl around!

MOSTLY F – you're high-achieving, high-kicking Suzie Bravo – the straight–A student of the A team!

MOSTLY G – you're Kimmy Beam, the best dog in the world.

READ THEM ALL